*A
Harlequin
Romance*

OTHER
Harlequin Romances
by LUCY GILLEN

1383—A WIFE FOR ANDREW
1408—THE SILVER FISHES
1425—GOOD MORNING, DOCTOR HOUSTON
1450—HEIR TO GLEN GHYLL
1481—NURSE HELEN
1507—MARRIAGE BY REQUEST
1533—THE GIRL AT SMUGGLER'S REST
1553—DOCTOR TOBY
1579—WINTER AT CRAY
1604—THAT MAN NEXT DOOR
1627—MY BEAUTIFUL HEATHEN
1649—SWEET KATE
1669—A TIME REMEMBERED

Many of these titles are available at your local bookseller,
or through the Harlequin Reader Service.

For a free catalogue listing all available Harlequin Romances,
send your name and address to:

HARLEQUIN READER SERVICE,
M.P.O. Box 707, Niagara Falls, N.Y. 14302
Canadian address: Stratford, Ontario, Canada.

or use order coupon at back of book.

A TIME REMEMBERED

by

LUCY GILLEN

HARLEQUIN BOOKS   TORONTO
WINNIPEG

Original hard cover edition published in 1971
by Mills & Boon Limited, 17-19 Foley Street,
London W1A 1DR, England

© Lucy Gillen 1971

SBN 373-01669-7

Harlequin edition published March 1973

Printed in Canada

CHAPTER ONE

THE long road seemed to wind endlessly on over the moor, and to Jane the country was not only beautiful but home. It stirred her imagination and brought back so many memories that for most of the time were almost lost. The moor rolled on into the distance as far as she could see, and she smiled over a childish delusion that it was the whole world and there was nothing beyond it but space.

It undulated mistily in the summer heat which shimmered like a veil over the lovely rounded hills of heather and bracken, here and there yellow-splashed with gorse and bound round with the hazy, silvery blue ribbons of streams and tiny rivers. Occasional outcrops of rock thrust their determined way through the close-cropped turf, yellowed in the summer heat but still looking cool and inviting like the beautiful wooded valleys that dipped modestly between the soft hills.

The moor never failed to enchant her and each time it appeared to her differently, as changeable in mood as she was herself. At the moment she had to admit there were other distractions that crowded into her thoughts and made her slightly less appreciative than usual.

It was two years since she had seen Gavin, despite the fact that they both lived and worked in London and really not so very far apart either. It was just that she had never been able to bring herself to act in what was presently considered to be a civilized manner. The break had been so painful that she had no desire to reopen old wounds by seeing him again.

She wondered briefly what Aunt Gaby would think of Peter, and admitted to a certain anxiety in that direction, for he was so different from the blithe, gay and at times autocratic Blairs. Aunt Gaby was, in fact, Gavin's aunt and her own stepmother, but she had been both mother and father to Gavin for many years while his parents were abroad and there was a rapport between them that was as close or closer than he had with his own mother.

Gabrielle Drummond had been a Blair before she married Jane's father, rather late in life. At ten years old Jane had been considered too old to accept her new stepmother as a replacement for her own mother whom she remembered quite well, so she had followed Gavin's example and called her Aunt Gaby, but the two of them had taken to one another at once and she had grown to love the small bright woman even more than the woman whose memory had faded with the quick, healing forgetfulness of children.

At first Gavin had resented her, for he was already fifteen years old and used to having his aunt's undivided attention during the time he was at home, but he had soon grown used to having her there and they had spent long school holidays exploring and making the wild plans that the young indulge in. He knew the moor from the time he was quite small and he was not averse to teaching Jane all he knew. Tragically Jane's father had been killed in an accident after barely a year of marriage to Aunt Gaby, and Gavin and his aunt had become her whole world.

It was two and a half years ago, when Jane was twenty-one, that Aunt Gaby had seen her most cherished dream come true, when they had come to her and said that they were going to get married. It was only six months later that a bitter quarrel had parted them, seemingly for good, and ended the engagement. Even now, the thought of Ellen Dray made Jane set her teeth at the memory of how she had come between them.

Ellen Dray who, as Ellen Dunn, had lived most of her life at Dart Farm only half a mile from Pendart, had always represented a threat but Jane had realized it too late. Ellen had married very young and left to live abroad with her husband, but not before she had tried as hard as she knew how to make Gavin notice her in preference to Jane. She had given up only when Gavin left Pendart to begin his career as an actor, a move which had proved well worth while. Then, two years ago, Ellen had returned to England, a young widow with a small son and an undiminished determination to attract Gavin to her.

She had been so pathetic and pleading, with her baby-blue eyes wide and tragic as she begged for his help. He was, she assured him, the only person she could turn to, and Gavin had been unable to resist the plea. Her father had left her no more than the old farm and her husband's estate was tied up in some legal tangle, and it was only for her little son's sake that she asked, she insisted, otherwise she would have managed somehow.

Gavin had fallen over himself to offer not only financial help but something more personal beside, and Jane still shivered when she thought of the ways he had been led into giving so much of his time and attention to Ellen. Jane had felt herself obliged to protest at last, and he had seen her protest only as jealousy.

He had accused her of being selfish and thoughtless and one thing had led to another until, finally, she had thrown her beautiful sapphire and diamond engagement ring at him and stormed off, declaring that she never wanted to see him again. They were both too proud to make the first move in a reconciliation and the time had stretched into two years, two years during which she had met Peter.

It was one of those strange confidences that can sometimes happen that Peter also knew Gavin, having met him at a business meeting some time ago, for Gavin, besides being an actor of some standing, had also inherited a good deal of his father's business acumen. He had various interests in different companies, one of them owned by Peter's father, and Peter himself was on the board so that they had come into contact with one another fairly frequently.

Jane glanced at the man beside her in the driving seat and wondered just what her feelings were for Peter. She was much more wary of committing herself to anyone since Gavin, but Peter was becoming increasingly earnest in his proposals and she knew that inevitably she would, sooner or later, have to decide what she would do about him.

It was always such a temptation to compare him with Gavin, and yet it was not really easy to do because they were so entirely different.

Gavin was dark, almost primitive in his ruggedness, with a piratical air of self-confidence that it was difficult to shake, and his expression changed as often as his moods, the deep grey eyes showing amusement, mockery and anger in quick succession, and he had a sense of humour that at times almost verged on malice.

Peter on the other hand was as fair as Gavin was dark and with his fresh complexion and blue eyes, far

8

less animated, although he was still self-possessed in a more reserved way. He had the sober expression and manner that befitted a business man of his standing, despite his comparative youth, and he seldom indulged his sense of humour. She had to admit to knowing him far less well than perhaps was wise for a girl contemplating an engagement, and it was this, as well as a natural caution stemming from her previous experience, that made her hesitate to accept his quite numerous proposals.

She would too have liked Aunt Gaby's approval of the man she proposed marrying and, since it could not be Gavin, Aunt Gaby would not be easy to please. She would certainly not take to Peter's rather serious manner, Jane thought with a sigh.

Hearing her sigh, and perhaps sensing her preoccupation, Peter Frith turned his head briefly and looked at her, smiling at what he saw. Jane always caused men to smile like that whenever they looked at her, not only because she was good to look at, but because she had a friendly, open face that invited smiles.

Her oval face had a loveliness that varied with her moods, but was always enchanting. Soft, red-brown hair swept back from her face into a thick cluster on top of her head and escaped into tendrils at her neck and forehead, and her greeny-grey eyes had a soft, shiny look, fringed with dark lashes. If there was the faintest trace of freckles on the creamy skin it was only during the hot summer months when she wore very little make-up.

Peter found her completely enchanting and could never get over how lucky he had been to meet her. He had been invited to what he had expected to find a rather dull cocktail party to promote some product or other and instead he had been introduced to Jane. They had talked for most of the time, never once mentioning the subject that was the reason for the party, but finding they enjoyed one another's company. There had been one rather awkward moment when Peter had mentioned Gavin and Jane had, in fairness, told him about her relationship to him and that he had once been engaged to her. He had been silent for a while, but Jane's assurance that she did not mind talking about him encouraged him, and they had gone on with their own private enjoyment in the midst of all the talk and publicity.

'There's a thoughtful silence about you,' Peter told her, breaking into her thoughts, and Jane smiled.

'This is my home,' she reminded him. 'It's always rather an emotional occasion when I come home; you must admit it's the most beautiful place on earth, isn't it?'

He smiled indulgently. 'If you say so,' he agreed.

It was more than usually emotional for Jane, for although she had been home several times by herself during the past two years, it was the first time she had brought Peter or any other man with her, and she was not a little apprehensive at Aunt Gaby's reaction to him. To Aunt Gaby he would appear as a substitute for Gavin and as such he would be judged harshly.

A signpost pointed rather vaguely across the open moor and announced the way to Penford, and Jane smiled involuntarily at the memories it recalled. It was on the edge of a tiny river just across there that Gavin had proposed to her, while they sat like two children by the water that sparkled and sang in the sun as it danced over the stones, and it was in a little jeweller's shop in

Penford that they had bought her engagement ring, laughing delightedly because the old fellow in the shop had not recognized Gavin's famous looks.

'Do we stay on this road?' Peter asked, once more breaking into her thoughts, and she shrugged off the memories that would keep crowding in, giving Peter a half-apologetic smile.

'No,' she told him, 'we turn off at the next turning, just past that milestone up there.'

He was silent for a while, taking the turning she had indicated and driving cautiously along a narrow lane that looked as if it might peter out at any minute. 'Are you sure I'll be welcome, Jane?' he asked, with an anxiety Jane shared in part, although she would not let him know it. 'I mean your stepmother, Aunt Gaby, didn't mind you asking me down here?'

'Of course she didn't,' Jane assured him. 'I told her I wanted her to meet you and she said to bring you for as long as you cared to stay. Visitors never worry Aunt Gaby, she enjoys company.'

'I feel rather like a prospective husband being brought home for parental approval,' he ventured. 'I only hope I pass the test.'

Jane hesitated, wondering how to tell him that so far Aunt Gaby had no idea how serious their relationship was, although she was astute enough to have guessed, Jane had no doubt. 'I – I didn't mention anything about – well, about you asking me to marry you,' she confessed, and saw him frown. 'I thought it best to wait until I could tell her personally, Peter. You *do* understand, don't you?'

He smiled wryly, flicking her a brief glance. 'I quite understand, darling,' he told her. 'I have to be approved first, is that it?'

'No! No, it isn't like that, Peter.' She looked at him reproachfully, wondering if he was going to be very resentful of her reticence. 'It's just that – that I don't know for sure how I feel myself yet and I don't want to commit myself until I'm absolutely sure.'

He nodded understanding. 'Yes, of course you don't, Jane, I'm sorry. I should have realized that with the experience you've had it will be a case of once bitten, twice shy; it's quite understandable in the circumstances.'

'Something like that,' she admitted cautiously. She had told Peter something of how she and Gavin had broken up, but she had not gone into all the details; it was still a private and personal thing and she did not feel close enough to Peter yet to let him know how deeply it had hurt her.

'I'm looking forward to meeting your stepmother,' he remarked. 'She sounds quite a woman from what you've told me of her.'

'She is,' Jane agreed softly, 'she's a very wonderful woman, both Gavin and I owe her a lot.' It seemed strange to bracket herself with Gavin again, strange and oddly disturbing.

'You were brought up together, you and Gavin?'

Jane hesitated. It was not so easy talking about the old times and about Gavin, not so easy as she had anticipated, but it was a peculiar and unexpected shyness that made her reticent, not bitterness. 'I was ten when I came to Pendart,' she said, 'but we spent all our school holidays with Aunt Gaby and sometimes week-ends too when it was allowed. It was home to us both.'

'She must have been quite remarkable to have taken on two of you,' he told her. 'There are not many women who would have done it.'

'She loved us,' Jane stated simply.

'She must have done, I can't wait to meet her.' He turned a smile on her. 'And I shall love her for just having made such a good job of you, my darling.'

'You *will* love her,' Jane promised, 'everyone does.'

His laugh was short and nervous and she noticed that his knuckles showed white where he gripped the steering wheel. 'I rather have the feeling,' he told her, 'that it's even more important that she likes me, isn't it?'

'Of course she'll like you,' Jane promised rather rashly, 'and so will Uncle Robert.'

'Uncle Robert?' He looked momentarily startled. 'Is there someone else staying there too?'

'Uncle Robert lives there,' Jane laughed, 'and you needn't look so scared, he won't eat you. Actually he's very sweet. I like Uncle Robert.'

'Oh of course.' Peter sounded almost as if he was speaking more to himself than to Jane. 'Sir Robert Blair, chairman of Blair Industries and Gavin's father.'

'That's right,' Jane nodded, 'but as I say he won't eat you, I promise. The head office is in Exeter and he commutes from Pendart.'

'But it must be twenty-five or thirty miles,' Peter objected. 'It's a heck of a long drive every day.'

Jane laughed. 'Not the way Uncle Robert drives,' she told him.

The familiar grey bulk of Pendart was just ahead of them now, set determinedly steadfast amid the soft hills and vast rolling expanse of the moor, and Jane felt her pulse quicken at the sight of it. There were so many things she looked forward to when she came back to the old house, not least of which were Aunt Gaby's deliciously huge teas which were fatal to anyone's waistline, but completely irresistible, especially after hours in the open air.

Riding and walking were things which she had done since childhood, long distances that would have defeated many girls but which Jane tackled with all the enthusiasm of a country girl. It was what she missed most in London, that and the wide freedom of the moor. As they turned into the driveway of the house she realized with a start that she did not even know whether Peter rode or not, or even if he enjoyed walking.

'It's wonderful country for riding,' she told him. 'Do you ride?'

'I have done,' he admitted, 'but it's been some time now. The chances are much fewer in town anyway, and I'm usually too busy to stray too far out of town as you know.'

'Mmm.' She answered absently, her eyes taking in the mellowness of the old house, the grey stone seeming to absorb the sun and take on a golden look, while the long flat windows glinted and flashed like a myriad smiles. Tall trees dwarfed it and rustled a familiar welcome from the back of the house, casting cool shade over Aunt Gaby's well-kept lawn. Nothing changed at Pendart and it was all so familiar and so enchanting that Jane felt the old tingling glow warm her heart as she sat in the sudden silence when the engine was cut.

The door opened as Peter handed her out of the car, and a round, anxiously smiling face appeared. 'Hello, Mary!' Jane ran up the two wide shallow steps to the door and greeted the short, stout woman who held the door open.

Mary Dawes had been with Aunt Gaby for over twenty years; she had been married and widowed in her service and was now as much companion as housekeeper to her.

'Welcome back, Miss Jane!' Stout, friendly arms embraced her for a moment before she held her off at arm's length and studied her shrewdly. 'You'm pale-faced,' she accused. ' 'Tis that city air, 'tis no good to anybody, I say, and 'tis high time you came to us again so's we can build you up.'

Jane laughed delightedly at Mary's undiminished maternal instinct. She had been with Aunt Gaby when Jane came to Pendart first and she had made much of the pretty little girl, coaxing her out of her initial sadness and delighted when she learned to laugh and tease with Gavin. Mary had been as delighted as her employer when Jane and Gavin were engaged and just as upset when it ended, and she eyed Peter with a certain respectful hostility over Jane's shoulder.

'Mary,' Jane remembered suddenly, 'this is Mr. Frith. Aunt Gaby will have told you that I was bringing a friend with me. Peter, this is Mary Dawes, Aunt Gaby's housekeeper, companion, cook – oh, just about everything, isn't that right, Mary?'

Mary nodded agreement, her rather pale eyes still suspicious. 'That's about right, Miss Jane. Shall I take those cases, sir?' She relieved him of their luggage and stood it at the bottom of the stairs to take up later. 'I reckon missus can't have heard you come,' she added. 'She was in the sitting-room, but she's maybe gone into the garden for a minute.'

'All right, we'll find her, Mary,' Jane smiled, and the

housekeeper nodded, turning to take the cases upstairs while Jane led the way across the hall. She knew exactly how the room would look when she opened the door, and smiled her anticipation of the soft glow of sunlight that dappled across the room through the trees outside, and the coolness of the breeze blowing in through the open french windows. She sighed blissfully at the sense of peace the room always gave her and looked ouside for a sign of her stepmother.

Gabrielle Drummond had just left the shadows of the paved area in front of the french windows as the door opened to admit them and momentary surprise widened her eyes, then she smiled, and Jane could have cried at the comforting familiarity of it all.

It was nearly two months now since she had last visited Pendart and yet there was some small change in the small bird-like face with its bright, dark eyes, some change that showed in the few extra lines at the corners of her eyes and on the forehead below the thatch of thick white hair. It was with a shock that she realized that Aunt Gaby was beginning to show her age and even the few weeks since her last visit could make a difference, however small.

'Jane dear!' She was across the room before Jane had time to get more than a foot or two inside the door, hugging her tightly while the bright, dark eyes studied her guest over her shoulder, as Mary had done.

'Aunt Gaby!' Jane felt a ridiculous urge to cry as she was hugged and, as if she sensed her emotion, Aunt Gaby's hand patted her back soothingly.

'Welcome home, darling.'

Jane freed herself from the enveloping hug at last and turned, smiling apology, to bring Peter into the group. 'Aunt Gaby, I want you to meet Peter, Peter

Frith. Peter, this is Aunt Gaby.'

'Mrs. Drummond.' Peter was more than usually formal, but Jane suspected that he was extremely nervous and she put a hand in his to reassure him.

'How do you do, Mr. Frith?' A small hand was proffered, while the dark eyes studied him with unconcealed curiosity. 'Welcome to Pendart. I'm sorry I wasn't at the door to welcome you, but I had only just stepped out into the garden.' She waved them to chairs and smilingly nodded thanks to Peter's good manners in seating her first. 'Did you have a good journey?'

'Not too bad,' Jane told her. 'We avoided the worst of the traffic. It took us longer, but it was worth it – at least,' she cast a teasing glance at Peter, '*I* thought it was, and it was my idea.'

'Have you visited Exmoor before, Mr. Frith?' Aunt Gaby was intent on putting him at his ease and Jane blessed her for it; her kindness and good manners were instinctive.

'Only briefly,' Peter admitted, 'on my way to Minehead. It's very impressive country.'

'We think it's beautiful as well as impressive,' Aunt Gaby corrected him gently. 'I hope you'll take advantage of your visit to see more of it. It's a never-ending source of joy even to the people who live near it.'

'I'm sure it is,' he agreed. 'Jane tells me it's good riding country.'

'But of course, it's noted for it, as you'll know. Do you ride, Mr. Frith?'

'I used to,' Peter admitted cautiously, 'but not much lately, I'm afraid.'

'Well, there's no reason why you can't ride as often as you like while you're here,' Aunt Gaby informed him. 'We have quite a good stable and you're welcome to use the horses any time you feel like it. I love horses myself, but I'm afraid I don't do any riding now. I simply can't bear to part with them, that's why I still have them.'

'Of course if you prefer it,' Jane teased him, 'you can go and catch one of your own off the moor.'

'I think not,' he denied, answering her smile wryly, 'but I've heard of the famous Exmoor ponies, of course, who hasn't? I'd love to see some of them while I'm here.'

'It's quite exciting in the autumn,' Jane told him, 'when they're rounded up and taken into Bampton for sale, although I hate to think that it's quite often the end of their freedom on the moor, that makes me sad.'

'Jane's a sentimentalist,' Aunt Gaby confided with a fond smile for the weakness. 'Gavin was always teasing her about it.'

It had happened already, Jane thought ruefully; already Gavin had crept into the conversation as he inevitably would. There could be no avoiding the subject of Gavin here, for the house, the garden even the moor itself were reminders of him, and for the first time Jane wondered if she had been wise in asking Peter to come here. This was so unmistakably Gavin's home and, while it did not matter so much when she came alone, she doubted if Peter would find the ever-present subject of Gavin very palatable.

'I'm not a sentimentalist,' she objected, as if the mention of Gavin had never been made, 'I'm just a humane human being who's fond of horses, that's all.' It was an argument she had used against Gavin many times and she half-expected to hear his deep, teasing laugh greet her protest as it usually did; instead it was

Peter, far more cautious and practical, who answered her.

'I imagine there are points in favour of both sides,' he said. 'At least if they were taken away from the moor there would be regular feeding and grooming which aren't normally available on the moor.'

Jane made a grimace of reproach at him, then leaned back in her chair, relaxed and so glad to be here again that for a moment she forgot everything except the sheer pleasure of being home. She could see the garden from where she sat, the neat wide expanse of lawn with its flower borders and the tall shady trees that protected the back of the house from the worst of the winter winds.

'Oh, I love it here,' she said, 'it's so peaceful.'

Aunt Gaby laughed softly, her eyes teasing her. 'You only remember the summer,' she told her, 'not the way the winds blow in off the moor in winter and the way the snow cuts us off when the storms come.' Despite the teasing Jane knew that Aunt Gaby would have lived nowhere else but Exmoor. She loved it as much as Jane did herself, or perhaps even more.

'I still love it here even then,' Jane insisted with a smile, 'and anyway, the good times are the best ones to remember, aren't they?'

'Of course they are, dear, and we had so many of them, didn't we?' The dark eyes regarded Jane for a second or two in silence, her mind busy with the thousand and one memories they shared. 'It was such fun having you two children here.' She sighed, shaking her head. 'This house deserves children, it's far too beautiful and big for just one solitary old woman.'

'Nonsense,' Jane retorted, determined to change the mood. 'You *are* Pendart and you're certainly not old,

Aunt Gaby, you'll never be old.'

'I'll be sixty-one next month,' Aunt Gaby reminded her. 'Don't forget, Jane dear. I was several years older than your father when we were married.'

'Not enough to matter,' Jane denied, 'and Daddy adored you anyway, as I do.'

Aunt Gaby laughed at the extravagance. 'We were a mutual admiration society weren't we? Poor Clive.' For a moment the bright dark eyes were sad with memory, but she was not a woman to dwell on past sadnesses for long, especially with a guest present, and she turned a smile to Peter. 'I'm sorry, Mr. Frith, we seem to have strayed into the past rather, it's a habit one has when one's family visits. I'm sure you'll understand.'

'Of course, Mrs. Drummond,' Peter smiled across at Jane. 'I hope Jane will be patient when I take her to my home some time soon, we're a rather large family and there is always so much to talk about. I seldom see them, you see, because they live in the north of England.'

'It's sad to live too far away from one's family,' Aunt Gaby sighed. 'It makes one incomplete in a way, one loses that sense of belonging that is so important to us.' She smiled an apology for her opinion so openly expressed. 'I hope you enjoy your stay here, Mr. Frith. Pendart is a happy house and we like to see our visitors happy. If you like walking and riding you'll have a wonderful time.'

'I'm sure I shall,' Peter agreed, 'and I look forward to being with Jane for two whole weeks most of all, we have so little time together as a rule.'

It was the wrong thing to have said, and Jane saw the tiny frown of dislike that formed between Aunt

Gaby's brows. It was unlike Peter to be so indiscreet and she wondered if the remark had been deliberate, with the intention of letting her stepmother know how things were between them.

'Jane can show you the countryside,' Aunt Gaby told him, refusing to comment on his statement, and it seemed, judging by his answer, that Peter had decided to make no further remarks on the subject.

'I haven't any riding clothes with me,' he admitted, 'since Jane didn't see fit to forewarn me, but no one bothers quite so much these days, do they?'

'It seems not,' Aunt Gaby agreed, though obviously not in agreement with such laxity. 'One sees people riding in all mannner of odd things and I don't really like to see it. Only the other day I saw that girl from Dart Farm—' She may have sensed Jane's involuntary stiffening at the mention of Ellen Dray, or she might have suddenly remembered to whom she was talking; either way she stopped hastily and for a second or two silence hung in the air uneasily.

'Is Ellen Dray back at Dart Farm?' Jane tried to sound casual and hoped she succeeded.

'This last couple of months,' Aunt Gaby told her, obviously relieved at her acceptance of the fact. 'Just after you were here the last time. Her circumstances seem to have changed somewhat too, judging by what I've seen of her lately. How that happened I can't say, for George Dunn died as poor as a church mouse and I heard that her husband left her nothing.'

Jane stared resolutely out of the window, her features carefully composed. 'Perhaps she has some wealthy and helpful friends,' she suggested, and Aunt Gaby looked vaguely uneasy.

Tea at Pendart was a hearty meal and Jane and

Peter did full justice to it. The combination of French and Scottish blood that mingled in Gabrielle Drummond's veins made for a pride in a good table and good cooking, and all the scones, tea-cakes and pastries were home-baked and delicious. It was one of her pleasures in life to see her guests and her family eat well from the variety of goodies she offered.

Because of the huge teas, dinner was always a late meal, and well before it was time for it, Sir Robert Blair arrived, his welcome for Jane robust and hearty as ever. He greeted Peter with politeness but far less enthusiasm, and Jane hoped he would not let his characteristic bluntness lead him into treating Peter as the interloper he would inevitably consider him. The fact that Peter was a businessman, like himself, would help, Jane thought wryly.

The two men were still upstairs and Jane found herself alone with Aunt Gaby for the first time since her arrival. The dining room was smaller than the big sunny room they had been in earlier, but it was bright and cheerful and commanded an excellent view of the moor from its windows.

Jane accepted the sherry her stepmother offered her and perched on the edge of one of the chairs by the table as she sipped it. This room was dominated by a slightly more than life-size portrait in oils, and Jane found its dominance discomfiting.

It hung over the old-fashioned fireplace and showed Gavin, three-quarter length, in the role of Heathcliff in *Wuthering Heights*. The role was not one of his famous ones, indeed he had been right at the beginning of his career when he had played it, but the part had suited him so perfectly that Aunt Gaby had been wildly extravagant and persuaded Terroni to portray him as he appeared in the role. Something about the man and about the perfect blending of two personalities had appealed to the great artist and he had made it one of his best works.

He had captured to perfection the rather primitive dark looks that had made Gavin so famous since and which were so appropriate to the part, but at the same time had managed to incorporate the small laugh at the corners of the eyes and mouth that gave the mobile face life and character. The mocking expression in the deep grey eyes was there too and seemed to follow the looker about the room. It was perhaps not wholly Heathcliff any more than it was wholly Gavin, but it was a striking and brilliant combination of the two, and Aunt Gaby loved it. She stood now in front of it in an attitude almost of reverence, her smile wistful and a little sad, as it always was whenever she looked at the picture.

Jane had loved the portrait because it was so like the original, but lately she found its rather overpowering presence discomfiting and was uneasily aware of the painted eyes watching her with that gleam of mockery. She half turned her back to it as she perched on the chair and sought a subject for conversation that would banish Gavin from her mind at least for a few minutes.

'What do you think of Peter?' she asked Aunt Gaby, and the old lady turned and smiled at her, almost as if she guessed her intention.

'He seems very nice, dear,' she allowed, her eyes watching Jane shrewdly, but with a kindly understanding. 'What did you say he did for a living?'

'He's a businessman,' Jane replied. 'He's on the board of directors of his family's firm and he has an interest in one or two other firms as well. He's very successful and very respectable.'

'Oh dear,' Aunt Gaby teased gently, 'you make him sound very dull, darling, and I'm sure he isn't or you'd never have become so friendly with him.' She studied her for a moment in silence and Jane steeled herself for the inevitable question. 'You *are* very friendly with him, aren't you, Jane?'

'Yes, I am,' Jane admitted cautiously. 'He also knows Gavin, in the way of business,' she added, and saw Aunt Gaby's expressive brows rise in surprise.

'Oh, does he?'

'Yes. He also knows about – about Gavin and me too.' She tried not to sound defiant, but was afraid she did.

'I see.' The dark eyes were hidden for a moment by lowered lids and Jane knew that the hurt she felt at their breaking up was still there.

Jane put down her glass carefully and got up from her chair, taking the small, soft hands in hers gently, her eyes pleading for understanding. 'Peter's asked me to marry him, Aunt Gaby.'

The lids flickered upwards and the disconcerting gaze questioned her anxiously. 'Have you promised you will?' she asked.

'No – no, not yet.' It was Jane now who looked down at their clasped hands. 'I'm not sure enough yet, and this time I have to be very, very sure.'

A gentle hand released itself and touched her face softly. 'Then don't be in too much of a hurry, my dear, think about it for a long time, as you say, be very, very sure before you say yes, it can be for such a long time.' She sighed and looked up again at the portrait that watched them so mockingly. 'I never tire of looking at

24

this painting, you know,' she said softly, 'it's so very much like him.'

'Very much,' Jane agreed, and felt her fingers curl tightly into her palms when her hands were released and she lifted her gaze to meet the eyes of the portrait again.

'I always promised it to you when my time came,' Aunt Gaby went on wistfully, 'but I suppose you wouldn't want it now, would you?'

Jane did not answer, but suddenly the life-size face was blurred and misty and she realized with surprise that there were tears rolling down her face and plopping warmly on to her hands.

CHAPTER TWO

IT was another sunny hot day the following day, and Jane yawned lazily as she went upstairs to her room to change into sandals. She had suggested to Peter that they should go for a walk after lunch, perhaps as far as the tiny river that wound its way busily across the moor less than half a mile away. It was too nice to stay indoors and she was always ready for a walk on her beloved moor, though she suspected that Peter lacked some of her own enthusiasm for the pastime.

As she went into her room she heard a car stop on the drive and smiled to herself. Most people in the country now only worked five days a week, but even on Saturdays Uncle Robert had to show his face at the office, even for a short time. She looked out of the window just in time to see Robert Blair disappear under the narrow porch and into the house, smiling to herself at the boundless energy of her uncle.

It was from his father that Gavin had inherited his dark colouring, and Robert Blair's black head, even at something over fifty, was as yet only touched with grey at the temples. He was perhaps better-looking than his son, for the rugged unevenness of Gavin's features had come to him from his maternal grandfather and had proved an asset rather than a drawback in his profession. She could hear Sir Robert's rather loud booming voice as she changed her shoes and thought how fortunate it was that Gavin had inherited its power without its harshness.

She had always liked Uncle Robert and he had

always treated her with a rather touching gentleness, being completely unused to children, and especially little girls. He had seen little of Gavin during his childhood and had been inclined to be rather heartily friendly than paternal towards him.

Jane went downstairs again, ready for her walk, and opened the sitting-room door on her uncle's booming voice. 'Hello, Jane!' He always greeted one as if it had been months and not hours since the last meeting, and Jane smiled at him affectionately.

'Hello, Uncle Robert, you're an early bird today. Have you given yourself the rest of the day off? It isn't often you're here, even on a Saturday, at this hour.'

'Too hot,' he told her with a grin that always reminded her of Gavin and even more so today for some reason. 'I can't get used to this blasted humidity.' Grey eyes, lighter than Gavin's, looked at her for a second or two. 'You look as cool as a cucumber,' he accused. 'How d'you do it?'

'For one thing,' Jane laughed, 'I don't rush around all over the place. You should slow down, Uncle Robert.'

'Can't afford to,' he retorted, 'there's never enough hours in the day for me as it is.' He grinned. 'I'll slow down when I retire,' he promised.

'You never *will* retire,' Aunt Gaby informed him tartly, 'if you don't drive more slowly, Robert. You're a menace on the road.'

'Nonsense!' Her brother laughed at her fears. 'I'm as safe as houses, aren't I, Jane?'

'You're a very good driver,' Jane agreed with a smile, 'but you do rather treat the Penford road as if it was Mallory Park.'

'Jane!' He looked so reproachful that she bent and

kissed him briefly on his forehead.

'Sorry, Uncle Robert, you're really a *very* good driver.' He looked somewhat mollified at the assurance and Jane turned to Aunt Gaby. 'I'm going for a walk with Peter, Aunt Gaby,' she told her. 'We'll be back as hungry as hunters by tea-time.'

'How does your friend like Exmoor?' Sir Robert asked, and Jane hoped that Peter was not within earshot to hear himself thus described, although she felt sure he had not meant the reference to sound as disparaging as it did.

'He likes it very much what he's seen so far,' she told him, 'but there hasn't been time to see much yet.'

'A *close* friend, is he?' Uncle Robert had never been able to count subtlety among his virtues, but Jane knew him and merely smiled at the bluntness of the question.

'Quite close,' she agreed, and saw the look that Aunt Gaby exchanged with her brother. 'Now I'd better go and see what Peter's up to or it'll be tea-time before we start.'

Almost as if on cue Peter opened the door, smiling at her inquiringly. 'I'm ready when you are,' he told her.

'I thought we'd go as far as the little river,' she told him. 'The one that runs almost at the foot of the slope from the back of the house.'

'It's a lovely little river, the Medd,' Gabrielle Drummond informed him. 'It's quite small, but it's really very attractive, especially at this time of year. It's one of Jane's favourite walks down there, isn't it, dear?'

Jane nodded agreement, and the way Peter looked at her she guessed he knew who it was had shared her enjoyment of the walk before, but he made no comment on it. 'I don't mind where we go,' he told Jane obligingly. 'You're the expert, darling, I leave it to you.'

'Jane is quite an expert,' Aunt Gaby allowed with a laugh, 'but Gav—' She bit her lip hastily, sending a glance of apology at Jane.

'Gavin's the real expert,' Jane said quietly, guessing her intention and refusing to be put off by the mention of Gavin. 'He knows the moor from the time he was a very small child, every ridgeway and packhorse trail. He taught me a lot of what he knew, but I was an old lady of ten before I started to learn.' She laughed lightly and took Peter's arm as they turned towards the door. 'However, I promise not to lose us!'

It was wonderful to walk on the moor again, Jane thought as they went out of the garden and on to the open moor, through the knee-high bracken with a hundred different grasses and wild flowers growing unchecked in the rich earth. Foxgloves rose as tall as Peter almost, and Jane sighed in pure content to be back again.

Out of the clustering growth of bracken and its attendant flowers the turf was warm and springy underfoot with the soft prickle of heather mingled among it. They walked down the gentle slope towards the river that glittered invitingly in the sun, and suddenly everything seemed so much less troubling than it had been. It was a sensation that never failed whenever she came back to the moor, the joy of being there again and seeing the mixture of grandeur and prettiness that combined to make this one of the loveliest parts of England.

As far as one could see Exmoor rolled away into the mistiness of distance, the horizon hazy with the day's heat, a haze drawn from the rivers and streams that crossed it like scribbles of silver. The only clouds were stretched in long white ribbons across a jewel-blue sky and were almost completely still as if they had been painted there.

'Across there.' Jane pointed to where little patches of movement shifted against the dark green shelter of the trees in the distance and betrayed a group of red deer. 'And there.' She pointed across to the more open ground and the bolder, more arrogant progress of the moorland ponies as they sought fresh pasture. She smiled at him with shining eyes. 'We'll go and find them one day,' she told him. 'The deer and the ponies. They're not so easy to find nearer to – they're very good at vanishing.'

As they walked down the slope Peter reached for her hand and she felt a momentary skip in her heart as his fingers closed over hers, because Gavin had always done that self-same thing. She turned her head in response and wondered how long it would take her to get used to seeing Peter's more reticent smile in this setting instead of the secret, meaningful glow of warmth in Gavin's grey eyes.

'Isn't it wonderful?' she asked, more to break into her own train of thought than to seek his opinion.

He nodded, looking all around him at the browny-greens and the grey of the occasional rock, the feathery grace of bracken and the tight little pockets of woodland. 'It's magnificent,' he agreed, 'but rather awe-inspiring. I feel as if I've been abandoned in space.'

Jane frowned, puzzled by his reaction. To her the moor had always been so full of life she could not imagine it as just open space. Even in the depth of winter when the winds carried the sleet and falling snow in searing sheets of blinding fury across the vastness of it, it had a strength and a feeling of permanence that was reassuring.

'I've never thought of it like that,' she admitted, 'but perhaps it's because I'm so used to it. I know it so well I'm not overawed by it.'

'Maybe,' he agreed, a wry smile touching his mouth as he looked down at her. 'I hope it won't be too much against me if I admit to not being an outdoor fiend, darling. I can admire good scenery with the best of them, but I've no hankering for acres of open space. Perhaps I lack the self-assurance to feel at ease so near to nature, I don't know.'

It was a thought she had never considered before and certainly not in the light of Peter's lack of self-assurance, and for a moment she was silent, readjusting some of her ideas. It had never even occurred to her that there might be people who did not share her love of the freedom the moor offered.

'Are you sorry you came?' she asked at last, and he shook his head firmly.

'No, definitely not, it's very beautiful here and I just want to be where you are. Anywhere is ideal as long as you're there.'

'Oh, that's very poetic,' she teased him, laughing a little nervously at the sudden turn the conversation had taken towards his feelings for her.

He did not answer and she led him to the very edge of the shallow river that ran swiftly over its stony bed, clear as crystal in the sun. 'Is this the Medd?' he asked, and she nodded, looking down at the little river with a smile.

'It's pretty, isn't it?'

'Very,' he agreed without enthusiasm, and she

looked up at the fair, rather set face with its sober expression.

'You don't like it here very much really, do you, Peter?' she asked. 'I'm sorry, I shouldn't have asked you to come. I – I forget you're a town man.' In truth she had to admit that she knew little enough about him to know what his tastes were for certain. In town it seemed to matter less, but here one seemed so much closer to the true nature of things that every aspect of man was exaggerated.

'I told you, darling,' he assured her, 'I like the country well enough, although I wouldn't care to live in it, but if you're here then this is where I want to be. I had thought,' he added slowly and as if he was unsure of himself, 'that I would have you more to myself here with fewer people around us, but instead I seem to be further away from you.'

'But that's silly,' Jane protested. 'I've been with you every minute since we arrived, practically.'

He was silent for a moment, his gaze on the bright water. 'I've been with you,' he agreed at last, 'but – well, this is Gavin's country, isn't it? Everything we say or do, everywhere we go, it's always Gavin. It's as if he was following us everywhere, always with us, there's no escaping from him here. I hadn't realized how closely your lives had been, still *are*, linked.'

'I haven't seen Gavin for two years,' Jane said softly, hating to admit the truth of what he said, but unable to deny it. Her life was involved with Gavin's and always would be to a certain extent while they had Aunt Gaby and Uncle Robert to keep them a family still. 'Of course the house is – is full of him,' she went on, half to herself. 'It was his home as it was mine, for longer than it was mine, and Aunt Gaby is as fond of him as she is of me. You couldn't cut off either of us from the other because we're both so much a part of Pendart, but you don't have to worry about – about what happened before, Peter, ever.'

'I don't know that I worry about it exactly,' he told her, 'it's just that I wonder if I'll ever get close enough to you to mean more to you than all this,' he swept a hand round to encompass the vastness of the moor, 'or the Blairs.'

Jane was silent for a moment, reluctant to admit how near he was to the truth. She hated hurting him because she was very genuinely fond of him, but if he meant her to give up seeing her family and coming to visit Pendart she was very unsure of herself there. It would be too much of a wrench and, she thought, not strictly fair if he loved her as much as he professed to. 'Would you rather go back to town?' she asked, praying his answer would be the right one, the one she wanted to hear.

His fingers tightened on hers and he smiled down at her. 'No, of course not,' he assured her, 'that's the last thing I want to do. For one thing Aunt Gaby would never forgive me if I took you away again so soon, and neither would you. Anyway,' he added wryly, 'I'm not running away from Gavin Blair's ghost.'

She raised wide, green-grey eyes to him, grateful for his understanding. 'There *is* no ghost,' she assured him. 'Anything between Gavin and me was finished two years ago. I'm free, sane and over twenty-one,' she added lightly, and he turned her to face him, holding her arms and looking down at her with his blue eyes a little anxious as well as questioning.

'I hope so, Jane, I do hope so.'

'Of course it is,' she told her. 'Until I come here I

never give him another thought. Being here it's inevitable that he – he crops up in conversation, it can't be helped, but I never think about him otherwise.' That was not strictly true, but at least she could try and convince him that it was, even though she could not convince herself.

'Oh, Jane!' He held her so tightly that she stirred in protest. 'I love you,' he told her, with more fervour than he had ever shown before, his voice husky as if unaccustomed emotion almost choked him. 'I love you and I want to marry you, Jane. Don't say no again, please.'

'I have to until I'm quite sure,' she insisted, putting a finger to his lips to stem a threatened argument. 'I can't promise to marry you feeling as unsure as I do, I – I just can't, Peter, it wouldn't be fair to either of us.'

'But why?' he insisted. 'You surely don't think I'd do anything to hurt you like Blair did, do you? Oh, Jane, you can't think that!'

'I don't,' she denied, seeking words to explain her unwillingness to be committed again. 'Oh – call me silly if you like, but I just can't bring myself to take that step again without being very, very sure, and I'm not, Peter, not yet.'

'I see.' He sounded cold and stiff and his features were set in an expression she might, uncharitably, have called sulky.

'No, you don't,' she said a little crossly, 'you don't see at all, Peter. You only see that I've refused to commit myself and, like most men, you've taken it as a personal affront.'

He made no reply for a moment, obviously wrestling with his emotions, then he suddenly hugged her to him tightly, his voice muffled against her hair. 'All right, darling, all right, I'll be patient, only don't make me wait too long for an answer, because I love you to distraction and I'm *not* a patient man.'

She raised her head, a look of half-amused speculation in her eyes. 'I always thought you were,' she told him. 'I can see I have quite a lot to learn about you yet, Peter Frith.'

The next day, Sunday, Jane slept unusually late and woke to find the sun streaming in through her window, so far round that she knew she must be late and glanced at the bedside clock hastily. Half past nine!

She left her bed lazily and ran a bath, soaking luxuriously in the scented water, knowing she would be too late for breakfast if she did not hurry although no one was ever very early on Sunday mornings. She yawned, and remembered that something had disturbed her during the night, some sound she had been unable to identify and had been too sleepy to investigate. She had vaguely registered Aunt Gaby's voice lowered to a whisper, and the fact that it was just after one o'clock in the morning, but beyond that she had taken no interest.

It would be nice to go for a long ride this morning, she decided as she dressed. She would ask Peter what he thought of the idea when she got downstairs. A final flick with the hairbrush and she approved her reflection in the mirror with a nod of satisfaction. Green always suited her, and even after less than two days, her skin was already losing its town paleness and showing a hint of gold.

She was half way down the stairs when a movement behind her stopped her and she half-turned to see who was even later than she was herself. 'Jane!' Her pulse pounded raggedly at her temple as she stared at him, meeting the deep grey eyes unbelievingly as they glinted down at her from the top of the stairs, still with that faint hint of mockery in them even now.

He had changed so little in the two years it was almost unbelievable. The dark brown hair, almost black but not quite, still fell forward over one brow in a thick sweep and the fine lines at the corners of his eyes and mouth still gave depth and character to the mobile face.

'Gavin!'

He came down one or two more steps and she felt the ridiculously fearful pounding of her heart, fearing he might make the greeting more personal. 'You look as if you've seen a ghost,' he told her, smiling as self-confidently as ever and, to her relief, making no attempt to add a kiss to his greeting.

'I – I feel as if I have,' she said, trying to steady her voice when it would quaver and tremble as if she was afraid of him. 'How – how are you, Gavin?' It was two years, she told herself, and it seemed that all she could think of to say after all that time were mundane, commonplace phrases that meant nothing.

'I'm fine, and I can see you are.' The grey eyes studied her from top to toe in a way that would once have brought a laughing protest for its impudence, but which now brought swift colour to her cheeks so that she hastily lowered her eyes. 'It's been a long time, Janty.' The old familiar and exclusive nickname did nothing to steady her racing pulse and she shook her head in an almost involuntary gesture.

'No one said anything about you being here,' she told him, annoyed at the way her voice sounded breathless and the way her hands trembled as she clung to the banister rail.

He smiled, coming down the few remaining steps that separated them, standing close beside her now, his eyes both amused and sympathetic, a combination that aroused her resentment. 'No one knew until last night when I arrived,' he informed her. 'I hope I didn't wake you.'

'You did, as a matter of fact,' she told him, sounding uncharacteristically snappish and wishing she could carry off such scenes as this with the aplomb that some women did. 'It was one o'clock if I remember, one o'clock this morning, not last night.'

'Have it your way,' he said amiably, 'and I'm sorry if I disturbed you.'

'Didn't Aunt Gaby know you were coming?' she asked, still suspicious of his sudden appearance, and he shook his head.

'No, as a matter of fact she didn't, and I don't imagine she'd have told you even if she did, in case you high-tailed it back to town.'

'I might yet,' Jane retorted. 'How long are you staying?'

He shrugged. 'A week or two maybe, until we start rehearsals for the new show.' Dark brows arched expressively as he studied her. 'Anyway,' he added softly, 'why should it worry you whether I'm here or not?'

She bit her lip, uncertain and uneasy and feeling unnervingly vulnerable. 'It doesn't matter, of course,' she agreed, and added, almost without thinking, 'I'm not alone.'

He laughed softly, the warm, deep sound that she had always found so shattering to her composure. 'That dramatic statement is your way of telling me that Peter Frith is with you, I suppose,' he guessed. 'I know that, Janty. Aunt Gaby told me last night.'

'You – you know Peter, don't you?'

'Yes, I know him.' He eyed her for a moment, his expression both quizzical and amused. 'I wouldn't have thought he was your type at all, darling, too stuffy and businesslike.'

Jane clenched her hands tightly, feeling the blood warm her cheeks again as she looked at him angrily. 'I like Peter very much,' she told him, 'and I don't know how you'd know *what* my type is after two years.'

He eyed her again for a moment in silence. 'Has it changed so drastically in the two years, Janty?' he asked softly. 'I'm sorry.'

She felt ridiculously close to tears, though for no good reason that she could think of except the shock of seeing him again. 'I like Peter,' she repeated, a look of appeal in her eyes as she faced him. 'You won't—'

He put a hand on her arm, his smile as self-confident as ever. 'Don't worry, darling, I won't eat him.'

'You couldn't,' Jane retorted, her chin tilted defiantly at him, stung into defending Peter although he was doing no more than tease her as he had always done. 'Peter's nobody's fool, as you should know.'

'Not in business,' he admitted, 'but completely besotted about you, so I hear. I'm not blaming him for that,' he added softly, 'you're very beautiful, Janty.'

Why, she asked herself desperately, did he have to use that idiotic nickname? No one else had ever used it, or would have been allowed to, and it gave her a sudden surge of nostalgia that threatened her composure. 'You seem very well informed,' she told him stiffly. 'I didn't know you listened to gossip, you used to despise people who did.'

'I still do,' he assured her, 'but there are things one just – overhears.' The grey eyes regarded her seriously, seeking an answer and not a little anxious as to what it would be. 'Is it serious, Jane?'

'We – we can't stand here talking on the stairs all morning like this,' she objected, unwilling to be honest about Peter, but when she would have turned and gone he put a hand on her arm and stopped her.

'There's plenty of time,' he insisted. '*Is* it serious, Jane?'

On the defensive again, she lifted her chin and met his eyes squarely for a second or two. 'I – I don't know,' she admitted reluctantly. 'I'm not as easily persuaded as I used to be.'

She could have imagined it, but it seemed to her that there was as much relief as amusement in the smile that touched his wide mouth and crooked it into mobility. 'Once bitten twice shy?' he quoted, unconsciously echoing Peter, and Jane flushed angrily.

Anger sparkled in her eyes and made them more green than grey and her head was angled in a gesture designed to quell him, a gesture doomed to failure. 'Can you blame me?' she demanded.

'Janty—' The hand on her arm, the deep persuasive voice, both rang a warning bell that she did not ignore. Gavin, above all people, could charm a bird off a tree if he gave his mind to it, and Jane was in no mind to be charmed into anything, so she shook off the hand impatiently.

'Did you know Ellen Dray was back at Dart Farm?' she asked, and saw the flicker of annoyance that gleamed in his eyes for a moment.

'Yes,' he said quietly, 'I knew.' He was waiting, she knew, waiting for her to make the next move, and as she stood, uncertain and irresolute, she saw the deep eyes glittering wickedly. 'Your move, darling,' he taunted her softly, standing with his arms folded, leaning nonchalantly against the wall behind him.

She looked up at him for a moment, reminded of other arguments, arguments that had ended in the way that lovers' arguments invariably do, only this was different, this was more reminiscent of the bitter quarrels they had had over Ellen Dray. No apologies, no asking for forgiveness, no kisses to compensate the loser, only two implacable wills refusing to surrender to each other.

'There *is* no move,' Jane declared at last, 'except for one of us to go back to London, and that seems rather idiotic in the circumstances, doesn't it? After all, anything there was between us has been finished for two years now, we're still cousins and Aunt Gaby is the only one likely to be hurt if we behave like children, so—' She shrugged, and wished she could have sounded more convincing.

'That was a very nice little speech,' he told her solemnly, only his eyes betraying the amusement he felt at her effort to be matter-of-fact. 'Do you often get carried away like that?'

'I'm trying to behave like a normal, civilized adult,' she retorted, 'but I'd forgotten your twisted sense of humour.'

'Not twisted,' he argued mildly, 'only slightly bent.'

'Oh, *Gavin*!' She flashed her temper at him, her fingers curled tightly into her palms. 'You never take anything seriously, do you?'

'Not if I can help it,' he admitted blandly. 'I took some*one* seriously once and it didn't work out. *I'm* not so easily persuaded now either.' He quoted her own words at her, smiling when he saw her expression, as maddeningly self-assured now as he had ever been.

'You can scarcely blame me for what happened two years ago,' she gasped, prepared to argue the point in her own defence. 'Even you wouldn't have the temerity to do that, Gavin!'

'Why not?' he asked as if it was a perfectly logical question. 'It was you who hurled your engagement ring at my head and stalked off in high dudgeon, or whatever it is that offended fiancées stalk off in.'

'You – you—' She sought frantically for words, as frantically as she had sought them two years ago, end just as dismally failed to find them, solving the problem as she had then, by turning her back on him and walking away, her back stiff with indignation, flushing at the chuckle that followed her and made a mockery of her dignity.

CHAPTER THREE

JANE was relieved to find the first day with Gavin and Peter under the same roof rather less of an ordeal than she had expected; indeed it had all been so polite and formal that she began to think she had made too much of Gavin's being there. After all, two years should be long enough for any breach to heal and there was no reason at all why they could not all behave as reasonable adults.

Robert Blair seemed to have accepted Peter rather better than his first impression had implied, and they spent a considerable part of dinner discussing a project of mutual interest and in which Gavin too was interested.

'It'd be a good investment for a young feller,' Sir Robert informed Peter after they had discussed the subject at length. 'I shan't take on any more at my age, got enough on my plate now, but I'd recommend it to anyone with some capital and time to await developments.'

'I'll probably take your advice,' Peter told him. 'I think I might, as soon as I can while the price is right.'

Gavin arched a brow in query, looking at Peter across the table. 'Were you thinking of making a killing in time for a spring wedding next year, Peter?' he asked, and Jane felt Peter's resentment like a physical thing.

Peter eyed him in silence for a while, then he smiled tightly, flicking a glance at Jane as he answered. 'Yes, as a matter of fact I was,' he admitted. 'I intend to keep on asking Jane to marry me until she says yes.'

'And you think she eventually will?' Gavin asked softly.

'I think so,' Peter assured him, 'eventually. I usually get what I go after, you know. I'm a good businessman whatever else I'm not, and I shall keep trying.' He raised his glass and looked at Jane over its rim, the blue eyes glittering with a cold resentment that made her shiver. 'To you, Jane darling!'

'I'll go along with that,' Gavin told him, and he too raised his glass. 'Janty,' he said softly, and Jane felt the warm colour in her cheeks as much at the intimacy of the toast as the anger in Peter's eyes.

'That's a ridiculous name to call anyone,' Peter opined, his voice harsh, and Gavin laughed, watching Jane to see what she would do.

'I'm used to it,' she told him, trying to sound as if it was of no importance. 'It was so long ago that I've forgotten how I got it even.'

'Its origin is lost in the mists of time,' Gavin claimed extravagantly 'isn't it, Janty?'

'It was,' Jane retorted, 'until you resurrected it.'

'But you *do* remember how you got it, don't you?' he teased gently, and she frowned.

'Yes,' she admitted at last, 'I do.'

'It was a beautiful peasant girl who married a prince and lived happily ever after,' Gavin informed Aunt Gaby, who looked the most interested party. 'Actually her name was Janetta and she was in a book that Jane was reading once, I teased her about it and christened her Janty after the other beautiful girl and it stuck.'

'Just like a fairy story,' Aunt Gaby smiled mistily.

'But without the happy ever after bit,' Gavin re-

43

minded her bluntly, and Jane glared at him for being so thoughtless.

'Ah, but it so nearly was, wasn't it?' Aunt Gaby sighed wistfully, apparently forgetting Peter for the moment.

'If you'll excuse me.' It was Peter, on his feet and grinding out his cigarette in an ashtray as if he bore it some personal grudge. 'I have a couple of letters to write that must go off tomorrow.'

He was gone from the room before anyone could say a word, and Jane sat, rather dismayed at the expression she had glimpsed on his face before he went. The blue eyes, darker than she had ever seen them, and the fair features set in a look that was hard and resentful, almost cruel. It was a look that was new to her and rather discomfiting.

'I rather think,' Gavin said quietly, 'that Peter has made a strategic withdrawal to express his disapproval.'

'I'm not surprised,' Jane retorted, and tightened her fingers round the stem of her glass, refusing to meet the look that Gavin directed at her.

'I have a feeling that I'm being accused of something,' he remarked. 'Am I, Janty?'

'Don't use that stupid name!' She glared at him angrily across the table and Aunt Gaby shook her head.

'But it's rather a pretty name, darling,' she protested.

'It's a pet name,' Gavin corrected her, 'that's why she doesn't like it, isn't it, Jane?'

'I never have liked it,' Jane argued, thoroughly angry and wishing she did not feel so close to tears. It was ridiculous, she told herself, to get so upset over such

44

a trivial matter.

'Ooh, you fibber!' The accusation, as well as the meaning smile that accompanied it, did nothing to appease her.

'Oh, Gavin, if you don't stop—' She bit her lip, realizing that she had raised her voice more than she meant to and that Sir Robert was eyeing her angry face speculatively, exchanging a brief but knowing glance with his sister. 'All right,' she agreed at last, attempting to lighten her mood. 'I didn't mind it once, when I was a small child, but now I'm not a child and I'd be obliged if you'd stop using it!'

The deep grey eyes studied her for a moment in the same way they had on the stairs that morning, and the effect was much the same. 'I'll agree you're not a child any longer,' he told her quietly and in such a way that her pulse hammered wildly in her temple and the colour warmed her cheeks until she longed to put up her hands to them and cover them.

'I'm old enough to know my own mind now,' she told him, not knowing quite what she meant by the statement. 'I know myself better than I did two years ago.'

'And how well do you know Peter Frith?' Gavin asked. 'It's six weeks now, nearly seven, since you met him. If you think you know him, darling, you've made a big mistake. You've only just scraped the surface. Our Peter's deep and not, you'll find, as pliable and patient as you seem to think. I'll say one thing for him,' he added dryly, 'he's a much faster worker than I'd have given him credit for – he doesn't believe in wasting time, does he?'

Jane refused to answer, to be drawn into further controversy with him; instead she got up from the table, her eyes hidden by the long sweep of lashes, the flush still colouring her cheeks. 'I think I'll go for a little walk while Peter writes his letters,' she told Aunt Gaby. 'I can do with some fresh air.'

'I was thinking of going down to the Dart for a drink later on,' Gavin told her, apparently abandoning his teasing for the time being. 'Would you and Peter like to join me?'

It was a flag of truce, Jane knew well enough, and she felt a little guilty for not accepting it as such, but she could not face another scene between him and Peter and she felt it was inevitable somehow if they were together.

'I don't think so, thank you,' she told him, and saw the slight crook of his mouth at her refusal.

'Suit yourself,' he shrugged with such an air of pathos that she felt more guilty than ever, and only just reminded herself in time that Gavin was an actor and a very good one.

She looked in on Peter to see how he was getting on with his letter-writing before she went out, and he seemed quite happy that she should go out for a walk alone, much to her relief, for she half expected him to raise some objection while Gavin was still around.

She walked out on to the soft springiness of the turf and heather, curling her sandalled toes luxuriously in its prickly warmth. It was almost dark and silent now that the birds were still, and even the breeze made little sound where there were no trees, only a soft whispering sigh through the heather and the bracken.

The sun was almost gone and with it the soft myriad of colours in the sky, leaving only a deep, full blueness that held the warmth of the day like an apple in a handkerchief. It was not so often that she had been on the moor alone at this time of evening, although she thought it the most beautiful time to come, just as the day was dying and the night starting its own new lease of life, a crescent of moon slowly gathering strength.

She walked down as far as the tiny Medd and thought how lovely it looked sparkling still with some luminescence of its own. Even the water was quite warm as she crossed it, shallow enough not to cover her ankles, and she walked on, almost forgetting how late it was. It was not until she felt the dampness underfoot and saw the soft whiteness of cotton grass that she realized in which direction she had come.

There was a patch of bog right over to the right, near one of the old pack-pony trails, and she had walked into it without noticing and without realizing where she was. There was really no excuse for her carelessness and no doubt Gavin would have called her all manner of derogatory names, but she would have been quite glad to see him at the moment, for it was dangerous to stray on to the bog at any time, but at least in the daytime one could see the safe way to take; now she could see only the white waving fluffiness of the cotton grass all around her and feel the ever-increasing yield of the ground under her feet; the pale light of the young moon was no help at all.

It was seldom the moor frightened her, for she loved every aspect of it, but the thought of the bog and the darkness combined made her bite her lip in despair at her own foolishness. She looked back to try and determine the way she had come and perhaps try to follow it back on to firm ground. At least she had not come very far into it, but far enough in the circumstances.

She took a cautious step to her right and with more

luck than good judgment stepped on to a patch of the long grass that formed a safe landing ground. It would be lucky if she did the same thing again, but she had to try and she stepped again, cautiously as before, only to draw back hastily as her foot sank almost ankle-deep into soft mud.

She stood there, trembling like a leaf and ashamed of how nervous she felt, frightened and uncertain, and for the first time feeling antagonism towards her beloved moor. 'Gavin!' She might have been a child again and calling for him to help her, only she knew quite well that he would not hear her this time because he was in all probability either on his way to the Dart or already sitting in the tiny public bar, relaxed and unaware that she had got herself into such a state.

Only a soft rustling in the grass answered her and she felt panic rise up in her as she had never known it before. If only someone would miss her, would begin to wonder why she was gone so long.

She stood still, afraid to move, afraid even to turn in case she went into the bog itself, which could become deep without warning. A sound not too distant, like the clicking of stone on metal, drew her head round and she stared into the darkness, wishing there was more light so that she could judge the new arrival friendly or not.

A blur of darker movement against the sky showed at last and she almost wept her relief to see the silhouette of a man on horseback, a silhouette she recognized. 'Jane?'

She hesitated now that it came to the point. She had thought she would be glad to see Gavin, but now he was there, although she was unutterably relieved, she was also reluctant to face the inevitable taunting he

48

would indulge in when he learned what had happened. 'Jane!' There was such anxiety in the voice that she could stay quiet no longer and called out. 'Where have you got to?' he called, still at the edge of the waving cotton grass that beckoned with ghostly fingers in the moonlight.

'The bog,' she told him, her voice already sounding defiant as she anticipated his reaction.

'What!' He dismounted, she heard the movement as well as saw it, and stood at the edge of the treacherous area. 'Of all the stupid little—'

'Don't yell at me,' she told him, 'just get me out of here!'

'Hold on.' There was silence for a moment or two and then the soft yellow light of a torch shone along the ground, seeking the safe passage she had been unable to distinguish in the dark. He was with her in a matter of minutes and stood only inches away from her, his face just visible in the torchlight. 'Come on,' he told her resignedly, 'follow me, and for heaven's sake hang on to me tight or you'll get yourself in the mire well and truly.'

Once more on firm ground she released her hold on his jacket and stood by the ghostly shape of the grey horse, breathing rapidly and feeling almost faint with reaction. 'How – how did you know I was out here?' she asked, trying in vain to steady her voice.

'Your boy-friend,' he answered as he swung up into the saddle again. 'He told me you'd gone out on the moor on your own and he was a bit worried about you.' He put down a hand to help her up behind him, but she shook her head.

'I'll walk back,' she told him. 'You can go on ahead and let Peter know I'm all right.'

'I'll do no such thing,' Gavin declared stoutly. 'You get up here behind me and we'll go back together. That way I'll know you're out of harm's way and I can go and have my pint if the pub isn't already closed when I get there.'

'It will be, I expect,' she said humbly. 'I'm sorry to have been a nuisance.'

'So you ought to be,' he retorted. 'You of all people who's always boasting how well she knows the moor, and you go and get yourself stuck in the bog in the dark! Come on, up you come.'

She put her hand in his and climbed up behind him, sitting sideways on, her arms tight round his waist the way they had often ridden before but not quite in the same circumstances. 'Was Peter very worried about me?' she asked as he put his heels to the grey and they set off across the moor, the animal sure-footed and sturdy enough not to notice the extra weight.

'Worried enough,' he allowed. 'If he's got any sense he'll read you the riot act when you get back – and serve you right.'

'He won't,' Jane retorted, 'he'll be too glad to see me back.'

He glanced over one shoulder and she caught a brief glimpse of white teeth when he smiled. 'So am I,' he admitted, 'though it never occurred to me that you'd be daft enough to get yourself stuck in a bog, or I'd have been even more bothered.'

She decided that silence was the best answer to that and simply hung on as tightly as she could, resisting the temptation to rest her face against him only with difficulty, for it was almost instinctive when they rode like this.

Peter was waiting for them when they came into the

yard and he frowned over the sight of her clinging on to Gavin, reaching up to help her down. 'Darling!' He held her for a moment so tightly that she could hardly breathe. 'I would have come and looked for you myself,' he told her, and sounded quite apologetic, 'but I don't know your precious moor like Gavin does and I'd probably have ended up a casualty myself. You *are* all right, aren't you?' he asked somewhat belatedly.

Jane laughed, as much in relief as anything else. 'I'm fine,' she declared, and heard the snort of disbelief Gavin gave as he took the grey into the stable to unsaddle him. 'Well, I am,' she insisted to his bowed back as he loosened the cinch, and he looked over one shoulder and grinned.

'She damned nearly got herself killed in the bog,' he informed Peter, 'that's how all right she was.'

'Jane!' Peter's eyes looked horror-stricken at the information and Jane shook her head, glaring at Gavin's unconscious back.

'It wasn't as bad as that,' she denied, 'though I admit I was scared, more scared than I've ever been before on the moor.'

'You've never behaved so stupidly before,' Gavin told her bluntly without turning round. 'You must be going mad to have gone out there like that in the dark. What on earth possessed you? Or were you so gooey-eyed you didn't realize what you were doing?'

'Blair!' It was Peter who protested, his fair face flushed angrily. 'I'm grateful to you for rescuing Jane as you did, but that doesn't give you the right to talk to her like that.'

Gavin straightened up from his task, turning half round to face him, his eyes glittering darkly in the light over the stable. 'I rescued my cousin, not your girl-friend,' he informed him in a voice that Jane recognized as one on the verge of temper, it was so quiet it was deceptive, 'and I was talking to Jane like that before you even heard of her.'

'Peter—' Jane touched his arm, her eyes pleading. 'Please, let's go in.'

He turned, reluctantly it seemed to Jane, and walked across the yard with her and through the garden to the house, stopping them suddenly as they reached the back of the house, turning her to face him, his face ghostly pale in the glowing half dark.

'Jane!' She was prepared for almost anything but the sudden and unexpected hardness of his mouth over hers, and she resisted, instinctively stiff in his arms as he held her tightly.

'Peter—' She managed the one breathless word before he silenced her again.

'Oh, Jane darling, I love you so much.' He held her so tightly she could not move, his face against her hair, tense and urgent and disturbingly different from his more usual calm. Then she remembered the icy anger he had shown when Gavin had been taunting him at dinner, and wondered if she really knew him at all. 'I love you, my darling,' he whispered against her cheek, and she was appalled to find herself remembering another time, when Gavin had used those exact same words to her. It was wrong, she told herself, to think of that at a time when she should have been stirred to response by Peter's declaration, she should not have been hearing instead Gavin's deep, persuasive voice or the way she had looked up at him with shining eyes, all too ready to say yes when he followed the declaration with a proposal. It had all seemed so right then, so perfectly planned and right.

She managed to turn her head enough to see the rich blue darkness of the night over the moor and the stars just beginning to show their light. 'Please, Peter,' she begged softly, and knew it was neither the answer he expected nor wanted to hear.

He held her at arm's length, studying her face in the light that shone at the corner of the house. 'I was so worried about you, I nearly went frantic,' he told her. 'You know how much I love you, Jane, why do you answer me like that? Why, Jane?'

'I don't know!' The words were like a cry of despair in the darkness and she moved away from him towards the door while he still watched her, puzzled and not a little angry. It had all seemed so uncomplicated in town, Jane thought despairingly, seeing him fairly often, enjoying the very different things she did there, but here where there was so much more room to think, she felt horribly uncertain, and the fact of Gavin being there made it even more difficult, as he should realize.

She should not have put herself into a position where Peter would inevitably be compared with Gavin, where there was so much to remind her of Gavin's declarations and promises which were all too much like Peter's. 'I just don't know, Peter.' She turned to look at him in the yellow light from the lamp, her eyes big and shining. 'It was a mistake to come here, I think. I hadn't – I hadn't realized—'

'That Gavin Blair's ghost still walks the moors with you,' he told her grimly. 'I hoped I could banish him, Jane, but what chance have I now?'

'I'm sorry.' She was uncertain even who she had most pity for, herself or Peter. 'I'm very sorry, Peter.'

'So am I.' There was a trace of impatience as well as irony in his voice as he reached out and drew her into his arms again, 'but I've no intention of giving you up as easily as that.' His kiss this time was gentle and less passionate and he held her less possessively, but there was still no doubt that he felt just as strongly and his avowed intention not to give up very easily she had no difficulty in believing.

'There's a new moon just risen,' she told him as he released her, her voice unknowingly wistful as she looked up at the night sky. 'We should wish.'

He laughed shortly as they went into the house, his arm tight around her waist. 'I already have,' he told her.

Aunt Gaby and Sir Robert were both in the sitting-room when they came in and Aunt Gaby hugged her tightly for a moment in relief. 'I'm glad you're back safely, darling,' she told her. 'We were rather worried about you being out there in the dark.'

Jane explained briefly what a state she had got herself into and Aunt Gaby clucked over her concernedly. 'I'm quite unhurt, darling,' Jane assured her. 'And I certainly shan't do it again in a hurry.'

'It's most unlike you to do anything as – as unusual as that,' Aunt Gaby told her, and Jane laughed.

'Well, at least you're a bit more polite than Gavin was!' she told her.

Relieved to have her back, Aunt Gaby left for her bed almost at once and Sir Robert followed a few minutes later, while Jane and Peter followed more slowly taking a few minutes to say good night at Jane's door.

She had still not heard Gavin come in and Jane sat for a while on her bed without undressing, wishing she felt more sleepy. A book would help her to sleep, but she hesitated to go downstairs again in case Gavin came back while she was down there. In all probability he had called on old Danny Bell the local poacher and an old friend of Gavin's since childhood. They would talk well into the night if their previous sessions were anything to go by, and Jane decided at last to chance a meeting and go down again for a book. If she heard him coming in, she told herself, she could quite easily slip off back upstairs without his even knowing she was there.

There were shelves of books in both alcoves, either side of the fireplace, and she sought something from the contents that would act as a soporific. It was so silent and tranquil in the big room and only the light from a single standard lamp glowed softly over the shelves of books as she searched.

She could see her own reflection in the glass of the french windows, the soft light catching her hair and turning its colour to burnished bronze, her creamy skin pale although in truth it was flushed with colour from the sun. She half-turned from the bookshelves and put an involuntary hand to her hair, gazing absently at the reflected room around her.

It was good to be at Pendart again, even though Gavin threatened to make her stay less pleasant than she had anticipated. She adored Aunt Gaby and Uncle Robert and she thought they would not grudge her any happiness she could find with Peter if she decided to marry him, no matter how disappointed they felt that things had not worked out as they had hoped. Pre-occupied as she was, she heard nothing until the door of the room opened and Gavin's reflection animated the scene in the window glass, then she turned her head sharply and looked at him, wide-eyed and startled, over one shoulder.

His wide, good-humoured mouth tilted at the corners into a grin as he looked at her. 'I wish you wouldn't always look as if you've seen a ghost when I appear unexpectedly,' he told her, 'it's not very flattering.'

'I wasn't trying to be flattering,' she retorted instinctively.

His laugh trickled along her spine like a warning and she turned back to the bookshelf, her eyes blindly searching among the titles and seeing nothing but a blur of letters. She remembered her vow to retreat as soon as she heard his key in the door, but she had not heard him come in and it was too late to retreat now. She remembered too that he had come after her and saved her from a very unpleasant predicament and she had not so far expressed her thanks for his coming.

'I – I didn't thank you for coming out for me,' she told him. 'I'm grateful to you, please don't think I'm not.'

'Oh, I'm sure you are,' he said solemnly. 'Very formally so too, by the sound of it. You're welcome, Miss Drummond.'

She reached blindly for the nearest book and turned to go, but he stood between her and the door and too close for comfort, a wide grin in evidence as he looked at the book she had taken. 'Do you really find a book about business practice good bedtime reading?' he asked, and she looked down at it, biting her lip when she saw its title.

'I – I didn't notice what it was,' she admitted, and pushed it back on to the shelf hastily, searching for another and wishing desperately that she had never come down again.

'Don't let me frighten you away,' he told her, sitting himself in one of the armchairs, his long legs crossed at the knees as he sprawled inelegantly low. One hand supported his chin and his eyes surveyed her speculatively. 'Are you seriously going to marry Peter Frith?' he asked bluntly as she took another book and prepared to go.

She stared at him for a moment uncertainly, wondering if he had seen her with Peter in the garden earlier and thinking it unlikely. 'I might – he's asked me to,' she admitted, and his eyes mocked her reticence.

'You haven't committed yourself yet?'

'No, I haven't.'

He smiled at her, steepling his fingers and resting his chin on them, watching her steadily, and she could feel the urgent throbbing of a pulse at her temple as she stood there clutching the book desperately tight in her two hands, too indecisive to move on out of the room and away from whatever it was that held her there. 'I see,' he said softly.

'Do you?'

He got to his feet with one of those smooth, quick movements that were part of his attraction and always reminded her of the lithe strength of an animal. There was, she thought, a lot of animal magnetism about Gavin, and he knew how to use it. 'I think so.'

He came and stood near her, unnervingly close and towering over her, a glint of mockery still in his eyes but backed by a gentleness that disturbed her alarmingly.

'Gavin—' She took a small step back.

'You're too unsure of yourself, aren't you, Janty? Too uncertain whether you can live with that very efficient businessman.'

'He's not only that,' she argued, 'he's kind and understanding and he—' She shook her head on the rest of her words and his mouth tipped into a crooked smile that spoke volumes.

'He wouldn't take pity on an old friend and step out of line to help her, eh, Janty? He'd play it safe and let you have your own way all along the line. That's what you like, isn't it? Everything as *you* want it, and you fly off into a paddy if you don't get your own way.'

She had not meant to hit him so hard, indeed she scarcely realized she had put the thought into action until she saw the vivid mark of her fingers on his cheek and felt the tingling of her own palm. 'You did that once before,' he reminded her softly, 'and you know what happened then.'

'Gavin!'

She remembered only too well the last time she had slapped his face like that. It had been just before they became engaged and a silly quarrel had developed into something more serious, both of them saying things they were sorry for afterwards. She had been losing the argument and, angered beyond endurance, she had slapped him hard as now. His response had been swift and inevitable and had brought the quarrel to a most satisfactory conclusion.

She moved across the room and reached for the door-handle as he reached for her, fighting against the once familiar strength of his arms as he pulled her close, his mouth hard and relentless and a little desperate, as if he knew what her reaction would be and he was determined to hold her there as long as possible. It seemed like an eternity before he let her go and the throbbing pulse in her head almost deafened her as she fought for breath, her eyes still angry but with a kind of desperate appeal in them.

'Jane!'

'No! Let me go!' She struggled free of him and he stood looking at her with an expression half longing, half exasperation.

A silence hung between them like something tangible and Jane longed to run out of the room and upstairs to the sanctuary of her own room, only a sudden weakness in her legs prevented her from moving as she sought to bring some order to her chaotic thoughts.

His laugh shattered the stillness and it had a bitter sound that she regretted more than she cared to admit. 'There's nothing so virulent as a woman who imagines herself scorned, is there, Janty?'

Jane could stand it no longer. Her self-control was crumbling fast and already threatening tears prickled her eyelids, while her hands trembled like leaves as she clenched them tight at her sides. 'I—' she began, then turned quickly when he moved towards her, and fled from the room.

CHAPTER FOUR

JANE thought it most unfortunate that Peter should have been called away from Pendart just when she needed him most, but the telephone call he received appeared to be urgent and he was required to leave almost at once. It would have been difficult enough facing Gavin even with Peter there, but with him gone she would feel more vulnerable than ever.

She walked out to the car with Peter when the time came for him to leave and he smiled down at her anxious face. 'You must go?' she asked, and he nodded, grimacing ruefully.

'I'm afraid so, darling, but I'm delighted to see you so reluctant to see me go.' He put his hands either side of her face and studied her for a few minutes in silence. 'Or is it because you're a bit wary of being here with Gavin,' he asked, 'without me to act as a buffer between you?'

'Perhaps a bit of both,' she admitted. That kiss of Gavin's the other night refused to be forgotten and she had not dared to mention it to Peter for fear of what he would do. 'Mostly,' she added with a smile, 'it's because I hate to see you go. I've so looked forward to being here with you and now you have to leave after only a few days it doesn't seem fair.'

'It's business,' he reminded her, and eyed her speculatively. 'You *could* come with me if you'd like to, I'd be delighted if you did.'

Jane shook her head. 'I couldn't do that, Peter, Aunt Gaby would be very hurt if I did.'

'Your stepmother,' Peter commented dryly, 'knows exactly how to get round you, Jane. You don't like doing anything to hurt her and she knows it. What's more, she'll stop at nothing to try and get you and Gavin together again – you realize that, don't you? That's what worries me, it's the dream of her life to see you and Gavin married and she'll keep trying, you know she will.'

Jane was uneasily aware that he spoke the truth and more uneasy when she realized that Uncle Robert would lend Aunt Gaby his support too. 'I know,' she admitted with a sigh for her own predicament. 'She seems to think I should have been more tolerant over what Gavin did, the way he behaved over Ellen Dray. She's just naturally more tolerant, I suppose.'

'You could scarcely be expected to condone him seeing another woman,' Peter retorted, speaking from what little he knew. Jane had never been very explicit about it to him. He lifted her chin and looked at her earnestly. 'Now don't let yourself be conned into anything, darling, not by Aunt Gaby or by anyone else, will you promise me that? If you feel yourself weakening, send for me quick and I'll come, business or not, and give you moral support.'

Jane could not repress a smile at the offer. 'I don't think I'll need to call for help,' she told him. 'I'm used to Aunt Gaby, but if I feel as if I'm slipping, I promise I'll yell for help.'

'See you do.' He kissed her lightly beside her mouth. 'I *shall* miss you in town.'

'I shall miss you,' she vowed and smiled up at him. '*You'll* probably fall in love with some ravishing blonde while you're gone and forget all about me, not come back to Pendart.'

'I'll be back,' he promised. 'I love you and I'm going to marry you one day, as soon as you'll have me.'

Jane regarded the fair serious face, her thoughts far away, trying to imagine seeing him every day for the rest of her life. Soon she would have to make up her mind one way or the other, give him a definite answer, and she hoped he would not take it too hard if she felt bound, eventually, to refuse him. 'You may have a long wait,' she warned him. 'Are you sure you want to wait?'

'Of course I don't,' he retorted, 'but I will if I have to. Whatever else I may lack it isn't tenacity, and I'll wait as long as I have to for you, Jane, I promise you.' He glanced at his wristwatch and sighed. 'I'd better go,' he said, and bent and kissed her again, this time more fervently. 'And no more excursions on to the moor at night,' he reminded her, and she pulled a face at him.

She stood on the drive and waved him out of sight, then turned back into the house. It was early in the day and although Sir Robert had already left for his daily trip to Exeter, Gavin and Aunt Gaby were still in the dining-room at breakfast.

Gavin looked up when she came in and grinned at her cheerfully. 'Have you seen him safely off the premises?' he asked.

Jane ignored the question and instead took the coffee pot from Aunt Gaby with a smile. 'Thank you, Aunt Gaby.' She poured herself a cup, trying not to notice Gavin's raised brows.

'You'll miss Peter,' Aunt Gaby suggested, 'won't you, dear? But still, it's not for very long, is it?'

'Two days is long enough in the circumstances,' Jane told her, 'and I shall miss him.'

'There'll be plenty for you to do with yourself,' Aunt Gaby consoled her gently. 'You're never at a loose end here, are you, dear?'

'I'm going riding later,' Gavin informed her, before Jane could answer. 'Will you join me?'

Jane shook her head after glancing at him briefly. 'No, thank you, I'm not really in the mood for company this morning.'

'What you mean,' Gavin corrected her dryly, 'is that you're not the mood for *my* company.'

'Have it your way,' Jane retorted, and he laughed.

'Peter wouldn't like the idea, hmm?'

'It has nothing to do with the way Peter feels,' Jane told him quietly, determined not to be baited into losing her temper. 'Why should he mind if I went riding with my cousin? You don't *have* to be so nasty about him, you know.'

His surprise looked genuine. 'I didn't know I was,' he objected, his eyes gleaming wickedly at her. 'But you were never short on imagination, were you, darling?'

'I do *not* imagine things,' she told him stiffly, following his meaning only too well. 'I'm merely observant, too much so for some people's comfort.'

'Here we go again,' he laughed, and Jane prevented herself, only with difficulty, from throwing her cup of coffee at his head, but the intention was plain enough in her eyes and he laughed again. 'You dare,' he told her a second later, 'you just dare, Janty, and you'll wish you hadn't. Slapping my face is one thing, but I'm damned if I'll have hot coffee thrown all over me!'

'You're an insufferable, conceited brute,' she told him through clenched teeth, 'and I wish *you'd* gone back to London instead of Peter!'

Neither of them were taking the slightest notice of Aunt Gaby and the old lady watched them with her bright, dark eyes sparkling as if she was enjoying their argument. It was rather like old times, Jane had to admit, and that thought alone was discomfiting, for she had no desire to drift back into the old ways again already.

'As I said,' Gavin remarked resignedly, 'here we go again.'

'Well, it's your fault,' Jane insisted, 'you started it by being nasty about Peter.'

He put down his coffee cup suddenly and leaned across the table, one hand lifting her chin roughly, his eyes showing exasperation as well as laughter. 'You're a bad-tempered little devil,' he informed her, 'you always were, and the last two years haven't made you any milder.'

She would have evaded his grip, but she could not, so she contented herself with glaring at him angrily. 'I wonder you have the nerve to criticize me,' she told him crossly, 'after the way *you* go on.'

He looked at her for a moment in silence, then the inevitable grin widened his straight mouth again. 'You brought up a real little firework here, Aunt Gaby,' he informed his aunt. 'You should have applied a slipper more often and cooled her down.'

'Gavin!' Aunt Gaby's reproach was mild and the bright eyes still held amusement as she looked from one to the other of them. At Jane rubbing her chin where his fingers had left their mark and at Gavin so self-confident and sure of the upper hand. 'You're being very unfair to Jane, darling, and you know I never spanked either of you. I didn't need to, you were both very good children.'

He sighed, leaning back in his chair, his eyes still on Jane. 'No, I'm sorry, darling, I shouldn't blame you for the nature of the beast. You did your best with both of us, bless you.'

'And you both turned out very well,' Aunt Gaby insisted. 'I'm proud of you both.' She glanced at her watch and got up hastily from the table. 'I really must go and see Mary before she goes shopping, I hadn't realized it was so late.' She smiled her thanks at Gavin when he opened the door for her, and disappeared in the direction of the kitchen.

Jane would have gone too, but he still stood by the door, regarding her thoughtfully, and she had no desire to get close enough to him to squeeze past. His silence had just begun to get on her nerves when he spoke, more serious now than at any time since he had arrived.

'I had hoped that in two years you'd have forgotten your – your bitterness,' he said quietly. 'I'm sorry I was wrong.'

'Bitterness?' she echoed, and laughed shortly to ease the tension she felt in herself. 'What bitterness? Two years is a long time. I don't even think about – about those times now. I'm older and wiser, but I'm certainly not bitter.'

'I'm glad,' he told her softly. 'You're too lovely to let anything eat at you for too long and turn you sour.' One brow lifted in query. 'Have you decided whether or not to marry Peter yet?'

'Are you going to marry Ellen Dray?' she retorted, and realized that she was not behaving as if she had no bitter memories of the past, rather the reverse.

His smile had irony as well as amusement in it. 'I

asked first,' he told her quietly. '*Are* you going to marry him?'

She hastily lowered her eyes, wishing she knew the answer to that herself. 'It's possible,' she agreed.

A hand, more gentle this time, lifted her chin to make her look at him and his expression could have been sorry or exasperated, she could be sure which, but after a second or two he shook his head slowly, a smile just touching his mouth. 'I wouldn't bank on it, darling,' he told her. 'I really wouldn't.'

'I won't be talked out of it if I make up my mind,' she insisted, a little desperately, and he was still smiling, his gaze resting disturbingly on her mouth.

'Who's talking?' he asked and, unexpectedly, turned away and walked out of the room, closing the door carefully behind him and leaving her with a curiously empty feeling in her heart.

The following morning, deciding that she would go for a ride, Jane was up earlier than usual, hoping, and succeeding, in breakfasting without Gavin being there. She would avoid him, she told herself, whenever it was possible, though at mealtimes it was almost impossible.

She walked down to the stable-yard separate from the garden and the house, and chose herself a rather frisky bay mare who shifted about in the most unco-operative fashion as she attempted to put on the saddle.

Once ready she set off across the yard, the mare anxious to sample the delights of the moor and skittering playfully over the cobbles. It was good to be riding again and the mare promised to be a good mount; it was an animal Jane had always liked and understood and they went well together.

For some reason Jane found herself dwelling on the thought of Ellen Dray this morning, though she could not imagine why this morning any more than any other morning. Unless it was because yesterday she thought Gavin had been riding with the other girl when he had invited her to join him; she did not know for sure and she could scarcely ask him in the circumstances.

It was still a puzzle to her why, when Jane had ended their engagement, Gavin had not married Ellen Dray; it could hardly be because of any reticence on Ellen's part, for she had never made any secret of her motives in that direction. It was possible of course that he too was being ultra-cautious before venturing into the field a second time.

Jane had realized long before now that she had played right into Ellen's hands by acting as she did; she should have stuck to her guns and made it more difficult for her, but her pride had been hurt and she, like Gavin, had a stubborn pride that would not be slighted. Anyway, she shrugged off the thought, it was all over now and she must make up her mind about Peter. The only trouble was that Pendart was the last place she should have come to make up her mind on that subject.

Once on the open moor she gave the mare her head for a while, enjoying the smooth speed of the animal and the tug of the wind in her hair. She wore it long today and not in its more usual formal style, and it blew out behind her as she rode, tossed and tangled in the wind, giving her a sense of freedom which she revelled in.

There was a promise of rain in the air today and a grey haze hid the distance, with cross-looking clouds scudding busily under a blue-grey sky. Gine Tor was the place she had in view and she hoped she could make it before the rain came. She crossed the tiny river Medd and one of the little streams that meandered all over the moor, heading for the great grey outcrop of rock that dominated the nearer scene and afforded a breathtaking view from its top.

It was quite a long ride but worth it, she felt, for the rewarding view; it was also a ride she had taken many times before with Gavin and its familiarity haunted her. The mare was a willing animal and flicked her ears appreciatively at the warm wind that held a promise of rain, maybe even a storm. It would not be the first time Jane had been caught in a summer storm, but today she had not taken her usual precaution and brought a jacket. If she got caught out here on the moor she would get very, very wet and she could blame no one but herself.

The rain when it came, gave warning with some big, ominous spots that made the mare shake her head protestingly, and it was only minutes before it was lashing down with such fury that Jane was soaked through to her skin in just a few minutes. The wind joined forces with it and together they did their best to sweep her from the saddle so that she crouched low over the mare's neck. Gine Tor itself was the nearest shelter and Jane put her heels to her mount, heading for the giant rocks that were already shining greyly in the near distance.

Gine Tor looked more manufactured than natural, and indeed it could have been left as a monument to Stone Age man, for it had stood in its present form for many hundreds of years, its twin rocks joined at their peak to form a natural arch. Another rock, standing almost as high, stood a little behind it and together they formed a cave-like formation that had sheltered Gavin and her several times. Jane headed for it now, unerringly, even in the stinging rain that half-blinded her, crouched low with the mare's ears flat and her pace eager as she covered the ground, hooves pounding furiously into the already soft ground in a kind of savage enjoyment, mane and tail flying.

Intent on holding the animal on course, Jane had little time to give to anything else, but gradually her attention was drawn to other sounds, just audible above the hiss of the rain and the drumming hooves of the mare. Other hooves were racing along behind her and she turned instinctively to see who it was.

A powerful grey, glistening wet, was rapidly gaining on her own mount and she had time to recognize the figure crouched low over his neck, the rider's dark face streaming with water but alight with the same kind of savage pleasure that drove the mare on. Even in the worst of a storm, Gavin could find reason to smile, and she saw the white flash of his teeth before she turned back again.

'Race you!' The words carried back to her on the wind as he passed her and again she saw the wide smile flash briefly at her.

Almost automatically she urged the mare to greater effort, her own hair flying behind her, as the animal's mane and tail did, the wetness of her shirt clinging to her body coldly and horribly cloying. The mare responded gallantly, but even so the grey was there some yards ahead of them and Gavin already ducked into the shelter of the archway.

He came out again as she arrived and took the reins from her, leading both animals round to the lee of the rock, away from the worst of the storm. Moments later he came back to join her, shaking rain from his hair and eyeing her amusedly. 'You usually have enough sense to bring a jacket with you,' he told her. 'You look like a drowned pup.'

'I don't doubt I do,' she retorted, 'but you don't look much better yourself, and you *could* have been more tactful.' She put a hand to her long hair, dripping water and clinging uncomfortably to her neck. Without warning he reached out and gathered the wet strands into a thick rope then, with both hands, wrung the water from it so hard that she squealed a protest. 'Stop it, Gavin, you're hurting me!'

'I'm only trying to help,' he assured her with a smile. 'You seemed content to let it drip all over the place, it'll dry much quicker now.'

His own thick hair was as wet as hers and he shook his head impatiently, scattering drops over her. 'Be careful,' she protested, 'don't shake yourself like a dog — you talked about me dripping all over the place!'

He looked at her steadily for a moment, his eyes dark and amused. 'You *are* a grouchy little devil this morning, aren't you? Is it because you're missing Peter that you're such a little misery?'

She glared at him in meaningful silence for a second or two, then lifted her arms to pull back the long, wet hair from her face. 'It's because I'm wet and uncomfortable and also the company I'm obliged to keep that I'm a misery,' she retorted at last. 'If I *am* a misery.'

'Oh, you are,' he assured her cheerfully. The shiver that shook her body brought his attention to her wet clothes. 'You'd beter get that shirt off,' he told her brusquely, 'it's soaking wet and you'll catch your death

70

standing there.' He was already taking off his jacket, the rough tweed far less wet than the thin shirt she wore. 'Come on,' he added impatiently when she hesitated.

'I'm all right,' she insisted stubbornly, and leaned against the cold rock as far away from him as she could get. There was little enough room between the two tall points of rock and Gavin was so tall as to make it seem even less.

He sighed exasperation as he regarded her for a moment, his eyes glittering darkly in the dimness of their shelter. 'Don't be such an idiot,' he retorted. 'Get that shirt off before you catch pneumonia.'

'I—' She got no further than the one syllable before he started to unfasten the top button of her shirt and she slapped at his hands angrily. 'I can do it,' she told him, and flushed at the deep chuckle he gave. She had never in her life felt so horribly vulnerable and she suspected he knew it.

'Don't tell me you're shy,' he teased her, 'not with me, Janty. I've seen you in far less, more than once, remember.'

'When I was a little girl,' she agreed shortly, 'and I'm not a little girl any longer.' She pulled off the dripping wet shirt and accepted the warmth of the jacket gratefully when he held it for her. The sleeves were about a foot too long for her arms and the shoulders dropped nearly to her elbows, but it felt warm and dry and she hugged it to her, glaring at him balefully.

'You shouldn't glare at me like that,' he protested. 'I *did* give you my coat.'

'Thank you.' She looked past him to the dripping landscape outside and thought that even in this

71

weather there was a kind of savage beauty about the moor. Almost involuntarily she looked at him, his head turned away from her, and thought how perfectly he fitted into his environment. The rugged, almost primitive features could have been carved from the rock of the tor and there was a savage strength about him that matched the mood of the moor. It was a comparison that made her shiver and he turned his head to look at her again. 'Are you still cold?'

'No.' She shook her head, remembering unwillingly the times they had been here before, with the rain pouring down outside and Gavin's arms round her as they watched the storm, their wet heads close together in the shelter of the rock.

He leaned against the rock beside her, his arms folded, completely at ease and with an enigmatic smile on his face that made her uneasy. 'You always manage to look beautiful,' he told her, 'even when your hair's in rats' tails and you've lost your shirt.'

The compliment and the look that accompanied it made her even more wary and she shifted a fraction of an inch further away from him, clutching the jacket to her defensively. 'Thank you.'

'Well, you don't sound very pleased about it,' he complained. 'Most women would relish such flattery. Most women don't hear as much of it, I suppose — that's the point.'

The temptation was too much to resist. 'Have you seen much of Ellen Dray since you've been back?' she asked, and he laughed softly.

'As much as you've seen of Peter, I suppose — why?'

'Oh, nothing, I just wondered.' She shrugged and grabbed hastily at the jacket as it slid down

72

her shoulders.

He eyed her speculatively, his hands in the pockets of his riding-breeches, his wet, dark head slightly to one side so that the inevitable flop of hair half covered his brow, and Janes turned her head away quickly in case of what he might read in her eyes. 'You're still jealous of Ellen, aren't you?' he asked softly, and she turned back sharply, ready to deny it.

'After two years?' she said. 'Is it likely? I recovered from that girlish infatuation long ago. I've other things to think about now.'

'Like Peter Frith?'

'Like Peter,' she agreed, and turned to look outside again. 'I think the rain's easing,' she added.

He laughed softly and, inevitably, argued. 'It looks as bad as ever to me. You can't wait to get away from this place and from me, can you, Janty?'

'I – oh, don't talk nonsense! Why should I care about being here with you?'

'Because we've been here before?' he suggested, and Jane wished she could control the dizzying throb of pulse at her temple and the nervous tremble of her fingers as she clutched the jacket to her.

'Now you *are* talking nonsense,' she declared firmly.

'Is it nonsense?' He put out a hand to touch the throbbing pulse gently. He had always teased her about it, told her it betrayed her feelings, and she wished desperately that he need not have noticed it now.

'Don't!' She turned her head sharply away from his touch and he withdrew his hand with a quiet laugh that told her he knew her reason.

'Sorry – I shouldn't trespass.'

73

She knew he still watched her, that he was probably waiting for her to rise to the bait of that last remark, but she remained silent and kept her eyes averted, staring at the slit of light between the point of the twin peaks and the single rock that formed the back of their shelter. 'Poor Peter,' he said softly after a second or two, and it was as if he spoke to himself rather than to her.

She did not question his meaning nor object to the motive behind his sympathy, but watched the diminishing rain through the slit, her thoughts racing wildly with a thousand and one things, none of them concerning Peter.

'It *is* slowing now,' she said suddenly. 'We can go soon.'

He was smiling amiably when she chanced a hasty look at him. 'I'm in no hurry,' he informed her.

'Well, I've no special desire to spend the rest of the day here,' she retorted. 'I'll be glad to get home.'

'Out of the way of temptation?' he teased, and she flushed at the uncomfortably near truth of the remark.

'Out of these wet clothes,' she corrected him. 'And anyway,' she added by way of retaliation, 'I think your—' She hesitated to be as blunt as she had intended because there was a look in his eyes that warned her she was possibly treading on delicate ground.

'My what?' he asked quietly. 'Do go on, darling, I'd love to hear you say it.'

'Well, I won't,' she declared crossly. 'You know quite well who I mean.'

'Oh, I know who you mean,' he agreed blandly, 'but what puzzles me is why, if you've forgotten about what happened two years ago as you claim, you get so het up about Ellen still.'

'I'm not het up, as you call it,' Jane denied, 'I just don't think – Ellen would take kindly to this situation.'

'She wouldn't,' he chuckled, as if the idea amused him, rather than worried him. 'Any more than Peter would.' His sigh as he heaved himself away from the supporting rock was pure theatre. 'It's stopped raining, we'd better go before we compromise each other.'

The rain *had* stopped when they left their shelter, but the sky was still too dark-browed to remain dry for very long and Jane felt a little guilty about wearing Gavin's coat, although it was warm again now that the wind had died down with the storm and he would not really need it. They rode in silence for most of the way, Jane uncomfortably aware of the amused glances she drew and determined not to turn her head and meet them.

'That jacket doesn't really do anything for you,' he told her suddenly, as they neared the yard at Pendart, and she tried to resist the smile that instinctively touched her mouth.

'It's warm and dry,' she said, 'and that's all I'm concerned with at the moment.' She chanced a quick glance at him and saw his smile. 'I'll give it back to you as soon as I've changed.'

'I hope your Peter doesn't think the worst if ever he finds out that you came back from a ride with me minus your shirt.' The deep grey eyes looked at her wickedly and she flushed.

'He won't know unless you tell him,' she retorted, 'and I don't think you'll do that, for your own reasons.'

'Maybe,' he grinned, 'but you'll never really trust

me, will you?' He did not wait for an answer, but led the way into the yard, dismounting before she could catch up and turning to take the reins from her. 'You go and make yourself respectable,' he told her, 'and I'll look after the horses.'

She relinquished the task willingly and went on through the garden to the house, going in the back door and through into the hall. Mary was talking to someone in the hall and it was only when the house-keeper turned towards her as she came in that Jane could see who the visitor was.

There was no mistaking the small, doll-like face with its huge round blue eyes and full mouth. Ellen Dray was much more blonde than any nature ever created and the full short style of her hair that rioted over her head added to the doll-like appearance and made her look deceptively childish, but there was nothing child-ish about Ellen Dray, Jane knew.

'Oh, Miss Jane,' Mary turned to her with every ap-pearance of relief, 'have you seen anything of Mr. Gavin while you've been out? Mrs. Dray was asking for him.'

The housekeeper noticed the grotesquely big jacket that enveloped her at the same moment as Ellen Dray did and the girl's baby-blue eyes narrowed sharply, her full mouth drawn into tight disapproval.

'Good morning, Ellen,' Jane said quietly, feeling horribly uneasy in the jacket. 'Gavin's on his way, he's stabling the horses.'

'You've been riding with Gavin?'

'Not exactly,' Jane demurred, thinking how Gavin's amusement about Peter's finding out had come home to him. 'We met while we were out.'

'And you got caught in that storm?' The voice was

high and sharp with antagonism and she made no attempt to return Jane's formal greeting, watching her narrow-eyed and showing a side to her nature that Jane was certain Gavin had never seen. Ellen was much too astute for that. Mary, Jane noticed, had discreetly disappeared.

'It was awful while it lasted,' Jane said, trying to bring the conversation down a level of normality; it was ridiculous to quarrel with the girl after so long, 'and I had to go without a jacket, of course.'

'It was fortunate Gavin had one,' Ellen said coldly, apparently feeling no such compulsion to keep things on a civilized basis. 'Is he very wet?'

Jane shook her head. 'No more than I am, in fact less. The jacket kept him dry and he insisted on my having it because my shirt was so wet.'

The blue eyes watched her like a cat, reading all manner of things into her simple explanation. 'I heard you were back at Pendart,' Ellen said. 'I understood from Gavin that you'd a friend with you.'

Jane nodded, wishing Gavin would come in and disliking the girl more and more every minute, afraid she would show it and only succeed in making things worse. 'Peter's a friend of Gavin's too. Now if you'll excuse me, Ellen, I'd like to get out of these wet things.'

But Ellen was not so easily put off, and eyed her shrewdly. 'I thought you were engaged to this – friend, or at least about to be.'

Jane frowned. 'Gavin appears to know more about it than I do,' she told her shortly, and would have turned and left her but for Gavin's arrival at that moment.

He came through from the back door with his wet hair flopping untidily over one eye, stopping short when he saw the visitor. 'Hello, Ellen, what brings you

77

here?' As a welcome it could be said to have lacked cordiality and Jane saw a pout purse the full lips of the other girl.

'That's not a very warm welcome, Gavin.' The big, baby-blue eyes were wide now and ingenuous enough to deceive anyone, not a sign of the narrow-eyed malice she had shown on Jane only seconds before.

Gavin put a friendly arm about her shoulders briefly and grinned apologetically. 'Sorry, but you've never been to Pendart before, have you? Is this a social call or did you want something?'

'You could say both,' Ellen pouted, 'but for the reception I got.' A glance flicked briefly at Jane put the blame for the lack of welcome firmly at her door. 'Actually, darling,' she added, 'I came to see if you had my car keys. I think you must have taken them with you yesterday, you dropped them into your pocket, remember?'

He struck his forehead dramatically. 'Damn it, so I did. I'm sorry, Ellen, I'll run upstairs and fetch them right now. Why don't you go and wait for me in the sitting-room?' He led her across the hall and into the sitting-room and Jane spent a moment wondering how Aunt Gaby would take her arrival, for she had never been very fond of Ellen Dray even before the break between Jane and Gavin.

When Jane came downstairs again, Gavin had still not put in an appearance and Aunt Gaby was being polite but not encouraging to the blonde girl. She looked up with a smile when Jane came in and Ellen too, smiled, though less amiably.

'Gavin appears to have forgotten my existence,' she laughed shortly. 'I was just asking Mrs. Drummond if I might see her roses, Jane. Perhaps you could take me and show me, could you? Gavin tells me they're very beautiful.'

'They are,' Jane agreed, wondering at the motive behind the request. 'I'll take you to see them if you'd like, Ellen.'

Her obvious lack of enthusiasm did not deter the other girl in the slightest and she smiled her thanks at Aunt Gaby, following Jane out into the cool, dampness of the garden.

They had walked only a few steps along the paved path when Ellen turned her shrewd, narrowed eyes on Jane and smiled coldly. 'You had nothing on under that jacket when you came in just now,' she accused, and Jane stared at her for a moment in silence.

'You're wrong,' she declared at last, 'but I had taken off my shirt, it was so wet that I had to. Unfortunately I've left it out there, and it's rather an expensive one that Peter bought me last month.'

'What a pity,' Ellen drawled, her eyes icy. 'You'll have to get it when you go out there again. How long are you here for?' she added.

Jane flushed at the temerity of the question, but answered it nevertheless. 'About three or four weeks,' she replied quietly, holding her temper with difficulty.

'But your – friend's gone back to London.' Jane followed the gist of the questioning only too easily. 'I do hope a promising romance hasn't been nipped in the bud, Jane.' The laugh that accompanied the words was harsh and brittle and the malice in the blue eyes was chilling so that Jane shuddered involuntarily.

'Peter and I are friends,' she told her, wishing her voice had more conviction. 'There's no more than that at the moment, Ellen.'

'Just as long as you have no ideas in another direction,' Ellen told her with chilling seriousness. 'That *wouldn't* work out, Jane, and I'd hate to think of you wasting your time again.'

Jane flushed, her hands tight curled in her palms, and she would have walked off back into the house, no matter how rude it might have appeared, but a hand gripped her arm and held her where she was, forced her to meet the chilling menace in the blue eyes. 'I don't think you should come here again, Ellen,' Jane told her, her voice annoyingly unsteady, and the other girl laughed, a short derisive sound that was completely devoid of humour.

'I don't have to,' she jeered. 'Gavin comes to me.'

CHAPTER FIVE

TRY as she would, Jane could not forget the chilling malice of Ellen Dray's voice when she warned her about getting too close to Gavin again, and she found herself wishing anxiously that Peter would come back again. It was with a sinking heart that she took a telephone call that evening, and she half-guessed what Peter was going to say even before she picked up the receiver and spoke to him.

'Jane?' His voice had a harsh metallic sound over the telephone and she scarcely recognized it.

'Yes, Peter, what's happened? I expected you back by now. Won't you be here for dinner?'

He sighed and she could imagine the grimace that accompanied his answer. 'I'm afraid not, Jane, I really am sorry, but this wretched business is going to take longer than I anticipated.'

'Oh no!'

Her cry was more dismayed than she realized and his voice sounded anxious. 'Jane, what's the matter? You sound – I don't know, almost desperate. You're not yelling for help, are you, as you said you would?'

Jane laughed shortly. 'No,' she assured him, 'not yet. It's all right, Peter, I'm just naturally disappointed, that's all.'

'Well, I'm glad to hear *that* anyway. Are you sure that's all it is? You sounded rather desperate just now, darling, and if you really need help I'll tell them here to go hang and come back to you.'

Her laugh was more reassuring this time. 'Don't do

that,' she begged. 'It isn't worth risking a tycoon-level crisis and a dash of two hundred miles just because I miss you.'

'It might be,' he argued hopefully, 'if you missed me enough to marry me.'

'I'm just feeling a bit sorry for myself, that's all,' she explained, making no comment on his speculation. 'Please don't do anything rash on my account, Peter.'

'Has Gavin been throwing his weight around?' He sounded ominously quiet and she wondered what his reaction would be if he knew about that morning.

'No,' she replied cautiously, 'it was – it was Ellen Dray. We had a not very cosy chat in the garden this morning and I'm afraid I got the worst of it. I'm not very good at holding my own in an argument. I'm too easily made speechless by my opponent's cheek.'

Surprisingly he chuckled. 'Poor Jane! Never mind, darling, I should make it back tomorrow or if not then on Friday, *if* your stepmother will have me, of course.'

'Of course she'll have you,' Jane assured him. 'She liked you.'

'Well, that's a step in the right direction anyway, isn't it?' he said. 'All I have to do now is try and convince her stepdaughter.'

'You'll try and get back tomorrow?'

'Of course I will.'

'Good, then I'll tell Aunt Gaby that you'll either be here tomorrow or Friday.'

'Jane.' Her fingers tightened involuntarily over the receiver as she anticipated his next words. 'I love you.'

It was a statement difficult to answer, especially as

82

Gavin had just come downstairs ready for dinner, a knowing smile on his face as if he knew who her caller was and guessed the gist of the conversation. 'I'll see you tomorrow, Peter,' she told him, and heard his sigh of regret along the line.

'I hope so, darling. In the meantime, think about us, won't you?'

'I will,' she promised, as Gavin walked past her and she saw one brow rise quizzically. 'Good-bye, Peter.'

Gavin had reached the door of the dining-room when she put down the receiver and he turned and looked back, waiting for her to join him. 'That sounded rather like marriage vows,' he told her when she came within hearing. 'I will.' He repeated the words with mock solemnity. 'You haven't done anything rash, have you, Janty?'

Jane flushed at his tone as well as the implication. 'I don't see that my telephone conversation concerns you at all,' she told him. 'It was private.'

'So I gathered,' he admitted cheerfully, 'but I couldn't help overhearing that rather solemn promise, and you did look as if you'd just done or said something you already regretted.'

'It was something I regretted,' she admitted, 'but not in the way you think, it was because Peter can't get back tonight. Anyway,' she added shortly as he opened the dining-room door for her, 'you shouldn't have been listening.'

'Not listening,' he denied mildly. 'I overheard, and I couldn't help being interested.'

Aunt Gaby and Sir Robert were already taking their pre-dinner drinks when they went in and they both looked up and smiled, guessing the dissension between the two of them and smiling resignedly over it.

'I thought Mr. Frith was joining us again this evening,' Aunt Gaby said. 'Was that him ringing just now, dear?'

Jane grimaced her regret. 'I'm afraid he won't be back until either tomorrow or Friday, Aunt Gaby. The business he was sorting out is taking longer than he anticipated and some further trouble's cropped up too, I think. It's maddening, but there's not much I can do about it.'

'What a shame, dear, I'm sorry you're disappointed.' But not sorry that Peter can't get back, Jane thought, wryly, following her stepmother's thoughts with no trouble at all.

'That's the worst of being indispensable,' Gavin observed as he poured sherry for himself and Jane. 'No wonder these business tycoons get ulcers.'

'Not all of them, Gavin,' Aunt Gaby corrected him gently. 'Robert hasn't an ulcer and neither have you, and you're both business men, aren't you?'

Sir Robert laughed, eyeing his son with mock derision. 'Gavin's only a dabbler, Gaby, he's not a business man.'

Gavin took the taunt with an amiable grin, raising his drink in a silent toast to Jane, something which had once been a small, secret intimacy between them and which now sent the colour flying to her cheeks as she met his eyes. 'I get by,' he said softly, 'but I don't claim to be a tycoon like Jane's Peter.'

'I wish you wouldn't call him *my* Peter,' Jane objected, hastily taking a sip and without returning the salute.

'Well, isn't he?' Gavin asked. 'He's come home here with you and he's been dancing attendance on you in town ever since you met.'

'That has—' Jane began, but he was intent on embarrassing her and went on as if she had not spoken.

'Also he wants to marry you, doesn't he? So that, in my estimation, makes him *your* Peter.'

Jane took a deep breath, determined not to lose her temper with him, although she was fast approaching the stage when she must, as he well knew. Her eyes sparkled angrily at him over her glass and her fingers showed white at the knuckles.

'Ellen Dray wants to marry *you*,' she pointed out as calmly as she was able, 'but I don't refer to her as *your* Ellen.'

For a moment she thought he would lose his calm, but after gazing at her for a long and disconcerting moment in silence, he raised his glass again, his eyes glittering darkly. 'You did once, darling,' he reminded her softly, and laughed as he added with deadly accuracy, 'and added the word precious for good measure, if I recall rightly.'

It was a point she could not argue with and she contented herself with a baleful glare that she hoped conveyed her feelings strongly enough.

Dinner was the longest meal of the day as a rule and, despite the bickering with Gavin, she found herself, as the meal progressed, enjoying the easy familiar routine of it. It was very like old times, except that Robert was there with them as he had never been in the old days.

She enjoyed the many topics of conversation that were tossed back and forth, and the feeling of security that Pendart always gave her still. The last of the warm gold evening crept slowly round the white walls, drawing in gradually as they sat over coffee. It had always been the nicest time of the day, she thought, and it still was.

'Are you going out this evening, Gavin?' Aunt Gaby asked as the two men lit up pipes and added the nose-tickling fragrance of tobacco to the smells of summer coming in through the windows.

'Mmm.' He sent a halo of smoke up round his head and leaned back in his chair, lazily. 'I thought I might walk down to the Dart for a drink. Will anyone join me?' The question was general, but his gaze was fixed questioningly on Jane.

'Not me, dear, thank you,' Aunt Gaby told him. 'I've never been able to recognize the pleasure of public house drinking, not for ladies anyway.'

'Bless your old-fashioned little heart,' Gavin teased her. 'No one takes any notice of ladies in bars these days.'

'Just the same, dear—' She looked at Jane, her smile half encouraging. 'But don't let me stop you, Jane dear, if you'd like to go. I expect Robert's going too.'

'I will,' Robert agreed, and looked at Jane. 'Why *don't* you come, Jane? No one will take you for a fast woman if you join us, even Gaby.' He flicked a teasing glance at his sister, who took it all in good part.

'You go, darling,' she said. 'It will make a change for you.'

Jane hesitated, wondering if it was possible that they would encounter Ellen Dray either en route or in the Dart, and uncertain what her reaction would be if they did. The temptation to visit the little old-fashioned inn was irresistible eventually and she nodded.

'I'd like to come,' she agreed at last, and did not miss the quite obvious look of satisfaction in the deep grey eyes that still watched her.

'Good girl!' It was Sir Robert who voiced his approval so fervently and she smiled when his hand

86

covered hers in an impulsive gesture of pleasure.

'To please you, Uncle Robert,' she added, so that there should be no mistake whose invitation she was accepting.

The Dart was well within walking distance along the narrow road that passed Dart Farm, and Jane felt very small as she set off with Sir Robert on one side of her and Gavin the other. Both of them were a foot taller than she was and both so well built that she felt as if she was in company with a bodyguard as they crunched their way along the stone surface of the road.

Dart Farm, a tall, rather gloomy-looking building set well back from the road, was already showing lights when they passed and Jane suffered a few moment's misgiving when she saw Gavin's speculative look, as if he would suggest calling in to ask Ellen Dray to join them. It was a gesture she was not prepared to support, but she knew that dissension on her part would in no way deter Gavin if he had made up his mind. To her relief, however, he either resisted the idea or it did not occur to him.

'Small windows in that place,' Sir Robert commented as they passed. 'They'd need the lights on early.'

'It's a dark place altogether,' Gavin informed him knowingly. 'Ellen's having the windows made bigger and opening up some of the smaller rooms to make more space and light.'

Sir Robert considered the information for a moment thoughtfully, evidently following the same trend of thought as Jane's. 'That'll cost quite a bit,' he remarked. 'I thought that gel was short of money.'

'Not any more,' Gavin told him without enlarging on his meaning, and Jane smiled wryly in the shadowy light.

'Perhaps she has generous friends,' she commented softly, and sensed rather than saw the look that Gavin directed at her.

'Dray was quite heavily insured,' he told her quietly. 'It took a long time to come through, it sometimes does, especially when someone dies abroad and in unusual circumstances, but the money's put her nicely on her feet now.'

'Lucky gel!' Sir Robert opined, and put a surreptitious and comforting hand down between them to clasp Jane's.

'You could say so, I suppose,' Gavin conceded dryly, 'if you consider being widowed so young is lucky.'

No one spoke again until they were walking in through the solid wooden door of the little pub, then Sir Robert looked down at Jane and smiled encouragingly. 'Shall we all get slightly squiffy,' he suggested, 'and shock Gaby?' As an effort to set the mood of the outing it was a brave attempt and Jane was all for endorsing the suggestion if only because she was already having misgivings about the wisdom of coming in Gavin's company.

'I don't think it's possible to shake Aunt Gaby, is it?' she asked. 'She's unflappable.'

Regardless of Sir Robert's suggestion, Jane drank only a little, but she was beginning to relax in the quiet friendly atmosphere of the old place when the door of the tiny saloon bar opened to admit another caller.

Her blonde hair was tied round with a bright blue scarf that matched both her dress and her eyes and the latter went unerringly to Gavin, while Jane's spirits sank to rock bottom at the sight of her.

'Hello, darling, I thought I might find you in here.'

88

A determinedly possessive hand slid round Gavin's arm and only then did she give any attention to his companions. A bright smile beamed up at Sir Robert, friendly and ingenuous. 'Hello, Sir Robert, I haven't seen you for ages, have I?'

'Quite some time,' Sir Robert agreed, his eyes less welcoming than his smile. 'May I get you a drink, Mrs. Dray?'

'Thank you very much, and please call me Ellen, it's so much more friendly, especially when – well,' she cast a small, secretive smile at Gavin, 'when I'm a close friend of your son.' She named her choice of drink, when Sir Robert made no response, but turned and looked at Jane with raised eyebrows. 'I'm rather surprised to see you here, Jane, I didn't know you indulged.'

'Sometimes,' Jane admitted, meeting the malicious gaze steadily. 'I'm a big girl now, you know, I'm allowed out with the menfolk for a drink.'

It was, she supposed, rather a spiteful thing to say, but she could not resist it in the face of that self-satisfied smile and the way Ellen had laid claim to Gavin as soon as she entered the bar. It was Gavin's quiet meaningful cough that remarked on it, while Ellen Dray merely smiled, a little tightly, as if she had not gathered her meaning.

'It's a shame your fiancé isn't here,' Ellen commented. 'It would have been a nice party.'

'You're mistaken,' Jane said firmly, feeling her anger getting the better of her at the deliberate misunderstanding. 'I'm not engaged to anyone, Ellen, but if you're referring to Mr. Frith, as I told you this morning, he's a very good friend, that's all.'

'Oh dear, and now I've made you angry. 'I'm *so*

sorry!' The baby-blue eyes looked wide and contrite and she looked for all the world as if she might burst into tears at any minute, Jane thought desperately, wondering how Gavin could be taken in by her show of childishness.

'Anyone can make a mistake,' she conceded.

'But I'm such a silly for forgetting things,' Ellen insisted, and pouted reproachfully at Gavin. 'It's Gavin's fault really,' she added. 'He told me you were going to marry this – this friend of yours, I'm sure he did. Please blame him, not me.'

'I don't blame anyone except myself,' Jane told her, and swallowed the last of her drink hastily. 'I'm sorry to break up the party,' she added with a determinedly bright smile, 'but I have a letter to write and I think I've had enough for one night.'

She saw from his expression that Gavin had seen through her ruse and she dared not look at the doll-like face of the other girl or she felt sure she would have been rude to her.

'I'll walk back with you,' Sir Robert offered immediately, but Jane shook her head.

'There's no need for you to, Uncle Robert,' she told him. 'You stay and enjoy yourself, get squiffy as you intended to.' She tip-toed and planted a kiss on his cheek. 'I'll be O.K. on my own.' She glanced briefly at Gavin and not at all at Ellen Dray. 'Thank you for the drinks, Gavin. I'm sorry to break up the party.'

'Are you?' The question surprised her so much that she turned again and met the challenging mockery in his eyes almost involuntarily.

'I – I do have a letter to write,' she insisted.

'Pity you didn't remember it earlier.' He swallowed the rest of his drink and resumed his steady gaze. 'A memory is so unreliable, isn't it? Especially one of convenience.'

For a moment Jane trembled with anger, seeking desperately for words to convey her opinion of both him and his blonde companion, then, finding none suitably expressive, turned and left the bar, the door sighing shut behind her.

She had been so easily roused, she realized ruefully as she walked back along the quiet, stony little road, and she should really have refused to allow herself to lose her temper.

It was not jealousy, she assured herself, it was merely that she had never liked Ellen Dray, even when they were much younger and the other girl had never liked her. The main reason being, of course, that she had set her cap at Gavin and looked on Jane as an obstacle right from the beginning.

Perhaps, if things had worked out— She sighed in sympathy with herself and tugged a twig of hazel from its parent tree, studying the round flat leaves in the faint light of a new moon before discarding it.

Jane was more than a little annoyed, next morning when she woke to find that she was still rankling under the memory of last night's episode in the Dart. Next time, she vowed, she would not allow herself to be drawn into losing her temper in front of Ellen Dray. Either that or she would retaliate rather than retreat as she had done last night.

Gavin, apparently interested, asked if she had managed to get her letter written, when they sat at breakfast next morning. 'It sounded as if it might have been important,' he stated, as if he still believed in the mythical letter.

'Yes — yes, thank you.' She gave all her attention to buttering her toast and did not look up.

'Can I post it for you?' he asked. 'I'm going out later.'

'No! Thank you.'

He looked briefly startled, then grinned at her across the table, ignoring Aunt Gaby's interested expression. 'I thought not,' he observed, as if his curiosity had been satisfied.

'Oh, you're so clever!' Jane retorted, being angrily lavish with the butter until Aunt Gaby put a staying hand on her arm.

'Not really,' he denied modestly. 'I know you, that's all, darling.' She made no reply to that and a moment later he looked up again. 'Are you riding this morning?'

'Perhaps.' She eyed him suspiciously, hoping he was not going to ask to accompany her. 'Why?'

'No reason except that I just thought you'd like to know you haven't to worry about the weather this morning. The forecast is bright and sunny.'

'Good.' She disliked the grin he wore as he drank his coffee. She hated what she called his complacent mood and the more so this morning because she was only too well aware that he was laughing at her.

'Is your—' He stopped himself and grinned at her apologetically. 'Is Peter coming back today, did you say?'

'I hope so. Today or tomorrow, he wasn't sure when.'

'So you don't want to stray too far from home in case he arrives, of course.'

'That's right.' She regarded him curiously for a second or two. 'Why are you so interested?'

92

'No reason,' he assured her. 'I'm curious.'

Jane frowned at him. 'So I've noticed,' she retorted, 'and I can't quite see why you should be, it's nothing to do with you. I know you're only trying to make me lose my temper by being difficult, but you won't succeed, not this morning.'

'All right, all right!' He held up his hands defensively. 'But if you're thinking of making Peter Frith one of the family. I think I'm entitled to a little natural curiosity, after all, I am your cousin, remember.'

'Only by marriage,' she told him, and saw the flick of surprise that crossed his face. It was the first time she had ever tried to dissociate herself from the family and she sensed as well as saw the hurt in Aunt Gaby.

'Are you disowning us, darling?' Aunt Gaby asked gently, and Jane shook her head, reaching to cover the old lady's hands with one of her own.

'No, of course not, Aunt Gaby, of course I'm not. You're my only family and I'd never disown you or ever want to.'

'Not even me?' Gavin asked, and for a moment Jane turned and met the deep-eyed gaze steadily.

'Not even you,' she admitted.

CHAPTER SIX

AGAIN on the Thursday night Peter rang, full of apologies, and told her that he would have to see her the next day and he could not possible finish in time to drive down to Pendart that night.

'Oh, Peter!' She could not keep the disappointment out of her voice, nor the hint of impatience. She was undoubtedly unused to having her plans upset and she took it badly.

'I'm sorry, darling, you've no idea how sorry,' he told her, 'but it just isn't possible for me to make it tonight. I swear I'll make it tomorrow no matter what crops up, even if I have to resign.'

She laughed, despite her disappointment. 'Oh, don't do anything as rash as that, please. I'll see you tomorrow.'

'Without fail,' he vowed, and she pulled a face, not thinking that he could not see her.

'I hope so.'

'I solemnly promise,' he vowed, and laughed. 'You know, darling, it's almost worth it to have you so obviously wanting me there.'

'Peter, if you're—' She left the threat unfinished and he hastened to reassure her.

'Of course I'm not staying away on purpose,' he said. 'I wouldn't, Jane, you know me better than that.'

'Yes, I do,' she admitted, 'I'm sorry, Peter.'

'I love you, you won't forget that, will you?'

'You keep reminding me,' she told him, half laughing. 'I can't forget it, Peter, even if I wanted to.'

'And you don't, I hope.'

She sighed, uncertain whether she was telling him the truth or not. 'No,' she said, 'it's very flattering to have someone in love with you, very good for your ego.'

She was aware as she spoke that Gavin was passing her and she glanced up in time to catch his eye and the raised brow that commented on her statement. He went into the dining-room and closed the door with studied care behind him, oblivious of her frown.

'Jane?'

'Yes, Peter, I'm sorry I was distracted for a moment by someone going through the hall.'

'Oh yes, it's dinner-time, isn't it?' He sighed and she could imagine the fair, solemn face showing its regret. 'I do wish I was there with you, darling Jane, and I'll move heaven and earth to make sure I am tomorrow night, or before if possible.'

'Good. I'd better go now, Peter. As you say it's dinner-time and I don't like keeping the others waiting.'

'Good night, darling.'

'Good night, Peter.' She replaced the receiver and only then became aware that Gavin had left the dining-room again and was standing just inside the hall looking at her.

'I'm not listening,' he hastened to assure her with a grin, 'but Aunt Gaby wondered if you'd be much longer.'

'I'm coming now.' She joined him by the door and was prevented from going in by his standing there. He made no effort to let her pass and she looked up with a frown. 'If you're all waiting for your dinner, you'd better let me go in,' she told him shortly.

95

'Do I gather that Peter's not coming back tonight?' he asked, without moving, and she deepened her frown at his curiosity.

'No, he's not,' she told him, 'but I don't see why you're so interested in Peter's movements.'

'Still too busy?' he asked, persistently, and she glared at him, her hands clenched tightly.

'Yes,' she retorted, 'still too busy. Now will you *please* let me past, Gavin?'

He shook his head, his expression drawn with regret. 'Poor Jane, I told you you'd have to get used to playing second fiddle, darling. These tycoons haven't much time for a romantic life as well, you know. You're in for a very dull time, you have my sympathy.'

'I don't need your sympathy!' She pushed determinedly against him and he yielded at last, grinning at her widely as she opened the dining-room door and went in, Aunt Gaby noticing her high colour and the sparkle of anger in her eyes.

'Is Mr. Frith still not coming, dear?' Aunt Gaby asked, handing her a sherry.

'No, Aunt Gaby. I've already had to explain to Gavin, though I don't see why I should have, that Peter is delayed, he'll be here tomorrow.'

'So disappointing for you,' Aunt Gaby sympathized.

'Oh, don't show sympathy, Aunt Gaby,' Gavin told her, 'or you'll probably be put firmly in your place as I was.'

'Aunt Gaby isn't asking a string of personal questions,' Jane retorted. 'Unlike you.'

'Now, darling, I'm sure Gavin was only trying to help,' Aunt Gaby chided her, hating as always to see Gavin maligned in any way. 'Why don't you two go for a nice long walk on the moor after dinner? It'll blow your cobwebs away and you know how you always enjoy a walk in the evening, Jane.'

Jane sat for a moment, sipping her sherry and contemplating what speculation her refusal to go would arouse. Gavin would be so certain that it was because she was too uncertain of her own feelings to go with him as she had so often done before. Aunt Gaby and Uncle Robert would probably think much the same thing, and there was little else for it but to agree to go to let them all know once and for all that she could take Gavin in her stride and not swoon away like a schoolgirl at the very idea of being with him.

She drew a breath to accept the idea, graciously, but before she could speak Gavin himself answered. 'It would be a very good idea, Aunt Gaby, but I can't take Jane. I've already got a date with Ellen, sorry.'

He was apologizing to *her*, and Jane clenched her fingers round the stem of her glass, her eyes flashing anger at him as if she blamed him for her embarrassment and not Aunt Gaby.

'I was about to say I'd rather not,' she told him, 'but since you're seeing Ellen it doesn't matter.'

'We're only going for a drink in the Dart,' he told her blandly. 'You can join us if you'd like to.'

It was too much! she told herself. He was actually offering to take her along on a date with Ellen, as if he felt sorry for her and could think of no other way to console her.

'No, thank you,' she told him, hoping she sounded as coldly crushing as she meant to.

Gavin left the house soon after dinner and Jane saw him go, determinedly uncaring, but wishing Peter could have been there to boost her flagging morale. It was unlike her to feel so downhearted when she was at Pendart, but then she had never been there at the same time as Gavin, not since they had broken up, at least, and she wished with all her heart that she had the strength of will to go back to town until he had gone. Peter, she thought, would be only too glad to have her again in his own environment.

She sighed and decided that she would go for that evening walk anyway, even if she went alone. In fact the mood she was in at the moment, she preferred her own company.

It was a cool, uncannily quiet evening with the stars already edging into the still sun-streaked sky, anxious to make themselves noticed. There was not even much of a breeze and the grasses were almost silent as she passed, only barely whispering to each other.

Instead of taking the walk down to the little stream she walked parallel with the road, using one of the numerous ridgeways or old packhorse trails that crisscrossed the moor all round its edge and cut across at angles or wound tortuously round patches of bog.

One such trail ran along as far as the Dart, and she was vaguely surprised to find that she had followed it as far as the back of the little inn, almost unconsciously.

The yellow lights from its rear windows sat cosily in the soft dusk and winked at her like an invitation, but she resisted the lure and turned her steps towards the road, meaning to walk back that way.

She crossed the path and walked alongside the inn, hearing the quiet sounds of human voices as she passed the side door. The Dart was never a noisy house. Out on the road, she crunched her way along for a few yards before deciding that the grass edging would make more comfortable walking, silencing her steps, so that she could now hear every rustle of the hedge and grasses.

Another sound reached her too, a short while later, the sound of voices and of laughter. The laughter she recognized and turned hastily to try and penetrate the almost dark, to confirm her own suspicions. Unless she was very much mistaken, the laugh belonged to Ellen Dray, and she had not the least desire to be confronted by the other girl, especially in the company of Gavin.

The high, though spasmodic, hazel that lined the road afforded some cover and she hastily sought a thick enough section of it to afford concealment, telling herself, meanwhile, that it was an idiotic thing to do but preferable to having Gavin see her and thinking heaven knew what.

The voices were nearer now and the laughter momentarily stilled, but she could hear the crunch of footsteps on the gritty road and stood behind her hazel screen almost holding her breath.

It was Gavin's deep voice that first formed words that she could hear and she found herself biting her lip, hating the thought of overhearing their conversation but unable in the circumstances to do any other.

'Does Jane know?' The high, rather drawling voice of Ellen Dray startled Jane with mentioning her own name and she unconsciously stiffened into a listening attitude on hearing it.

Gavin chuckled, obviously finding the subject amusing. 'Not yet, she doesn't, but she will soon enough.'

It could have been her imagination, Jane thought, but there seemed to be an edge of reserve on Ellen's voice when she spoke. 'She may not take it in the way you seem to think, Gavin. After all, she has that — what's his name? Peter Frith — in attendance now, hasn't she?'

'I think I know Janty well enough,' Gavin told her, quietly confident as usual, so that Jane clenched her hands at not being able to retort as she would have liked. 'She'll probably be furious at first, but she'll simmer down.'

'I hope so for your sake,' Ellen drawled, and still with that sharp edge to her voice as if something either worried or displeased her.

The crunching steps died away gradually and Jane left her shelter and followed on along the road, still walking on the sound-deadening grass, her mind busy with trying to puzzle out what it was they had been talking about. It was obviously something that concerned her, and she frowned over the idea of being discussed so freely with Ellen Dray.

She had gone a further fifty yards or so along the road and had almost reached the gates of Dart Farm when she saw the two figures standing in the sweep that started the drive up to the old farmhouse. Hastily she stopped in her tracks and held her breath, hoping she had not been seen, desperately seeking to find distraction when Gavin bent his head and kissed Ellen briefly before giving her a hug and striding off down the lane towards Pendart.

If only, she thought, she knew what it was that they had been discussing that concerned her! It was no use tackling Gavin with it because that would mean letting him know how she had hidden from them, and that would no doubt please him enormously. The idea of her skulking behind a hedge so as not to meet him with Ellen Dray would strike him as highly amusing and make her own position doubly vulnerable.

She sighed as she walked slowly into the gates at Pendart, seeing the light in the hall like a welcome, and the door slightly ajar. She frowned over the latter, disliking the implication that someone knew she was coming.

Aunt Gaby was ready for bed and Uncle Robert yawning lazily when she walked into the sitting-room. Gavin sat, low down in the chair as usual, his fingers steepled under his chin, his smile and his gaze speculative as he looked at her.

'Did you have a nice walk, dear?' Aunt Gaby asked, and Jane nodded.

'Yes, thanks, Aunt Gaby, but I went further than I meant to and I'm a bit tired.' She looked directly at Gavin, suddenly bold enough to discover the reason for that open door. 'Someone left the front door open,' she said. 'It was ajar when I came in.'

Aunt Gaby and her brother both looked so obviously blank about it that it had to be Gavin who was responsible and Jane looked at him inquiringly.

'I didn't want to close the door in your face,' Gavin told her, his eyes daring her to argue with what he said. 'You were so close on my heels it would have been very impolite.'

Jane flushed, unable to deny it, but wishing with all her heart that she had taken any other path but the one she had. 'Did you see me?' she asked, trying to sound matter-of-fact about it. 'I didn't know.'

'Twice,' he told her, so obviously enjoying her discomfiture that she could have screamed at him. 'The first time was just after we left the Dart, Ellen and I. You seemed to vanish into thin air, then I saw you again just before I left Ellen.'

'I – I didn't want to intrude.' It was not much of an excuse, but it sounded feasible, only his laugh made a mockery of her efforts.

'I've got sharp eyes,' he told her with evident relish. 'Ellen didn't even realize you were around.'

'You – you didn't tell her?' She could not think why that should matter so much, but it did.

He shook his head, smiling crookedly at her over his steepled fingers. 'No, darling,' he said softly, 'I didn't tell her, don't worry.'

'I'm not worried!' She made the denial sharply, aware of Aunt Gaby and Uncle Robert trying to appear uninterested. 'I – I just don't want you or Ellen thinking that I was – was playing some sort of I spy with you, that's all.'

'Oh, Janty! Would I think such a thing?' he asked reproachfully, and she flushed.

'As long as you don't get the wrong idea,' she said shortly, and covered a yawn. 'I think I'll go up. I'm rather tired and I'm sure I shall sleep like a log after that walk.'

She kissed Aunt Gaby and Uncle Robert, both of them walking to the door with her, then Gavin called and she turned reluctantly. 'Goodnight, Janty.'

The grey eyes watched her with an expression she found disturbing, half challenging and part something she dare not interpret. 'Goodnight,' she answered, and hastily went out and closed the door behind her.

After breakfast next morning, Jane decided to walk instead of ride, thinking she would not go too far afield since she had no idea just when Peter would be coming.

She set off towards the tiny river Medd, taking her

time and enjoying the warm softness of the morning. The mist still hung over the ground like a veil and the sun, still fairly low in the sky, shone hazily through it, giving the whole scene an unreal, slightly eerie look that fascinated her.

As she walked down the gentle slope towards the lower ground she saw a small figure ahead of her, wandering rather aimlessly along as if there was no hurry at all and she smiled at first at the miniature adventurer, then frowned curiously. The moor was no place for such a small child to play unattended; it was all too easy to get lost, especially in haze as it was today.

From what she could tell from this distance it looked like a boy, but shorts and cropped hair were no real indication. The child reached the river some time before she did and she saw it standing at the edge, gazing down at the clear water, probably fascinated by the movement of it.

It was not deep and no harm could come as long as the child did not attempt to do anything silly like wade into it, so she did not hurry down. It was definitely a boy, she decided as she got nearer, and his actions confirmed it when he bent and picked up a handful of pebbles from the bank and experimentally plopped them one by one into the water.

'Hello!' The blond head turned quickly when she spoke and there was a trace of guilt in the wide blue eyes that regarded her suspiciously for a moment before he answered.

'Hello,' he said, and held tightly to the rest of his handful of pebbles as if he was afraid she would take them from him. He was perhaps five or six years old and there was a haunting familiarity about the small, lightly freckled face with its huge blue eyes and mop of blond hair.

'You're a long way from home, aren't you?' Jane asked, and he nodded, looking down at his hoard of pebbles. She had made no move to take them from him, so he seemed to think it was safe for him to resume his game and he plopped another one into the water, watching the ripples spread towards the bank, distorted by the speed of the flow.

Jane picked up a stone and sent it after his, smiling at the swift, bright look of understanding he gave her. 'It makes rings,' he told her, tossing in another.

'I know, the only thing is you have to be careful you don't topple in when you throw,' Jane warned him. 'Do you often come down here on your own?'

He shook his head slowly, a distant look in his eyes. 'I'm not really allowed,' he confided, 'but I get tired of playing with toys, I like it down here.'

Jane smiled in sympathy with his preference. 'I used to like coming down here too when I was a little girl,' she told him, 'and I still do. I was older than you when I came to live here, though, I was ten.'

'I'm nearly six,' he informed her, not without pride.

He was not a big child for six and there was an air of pathos about him that Jane found touching. He looked a lonely child and not a very happy one, although that, with small boys, could be misleading she knew. 'My name's Jane Drummond,' she said, by way of introduction. 'I live at the house just at the top of the rise here – Pendart, do you know the one I mean?'

He nodded, a flick of wariness in his eyes that sat oddly on a child of his years. 'I'm Alexander Dray,' he volunteered, managing his long name quite well, and Jane realized why his looks had been so familiar. Ellen

Dray's son was exactly like her, both in features and colouring, except that any freckles on her skin were always carefully disguised with make-up.

'Do you live with Gavin?' he asked with daunting bluntness and, Jane stared at him for a moment before answering.

'Gavin Blair?' She gave herself time to recover. 'Mr. Blair is my cousin and we're both staying with Mrs. Drummond and Sir Robert Blair. Do you know them too?'

'I've seen Mrs. Drummond,' he admitted. 'She gave me two shillings once when we saw her in Penford.'

Jane could well imagine Aunt Gaby's soft heart being touched by this fair, rather pathetic child, and she smiled. 'Mrs. Drummond's my stepmother,' she informed the boy. 'She's very nice, isn't she?'

'So's Gavin,' Alexander declared, evidently bent on seeing fair play.

'Oh yes, he is.' Jane felt that not to agree would have brought communication to an end and she quite liked Ellen Dray's son, even though he looked so much like his mother.

'He's going to be my daddy,' Alexander announced firmly, and frowned curiously when Jane stared at him open-mouthed.

'Is – is he?' she managed at last. 'Who told you that?'

'Mummy.'

So that, thought Jane dizzily, was what that conversation had been about last night. Gavin had been so sure that she was still interested enough in him to be-furious when she heard he was at last going to marry Ellen Dray. She brought herself back to reality when she realized that the boy was watching her curiously, obviously puzzled by her reaction to his news.

'I see,' she said, hoping she sounded normally interested and no more than that. 'Well, you're a very lucky litle boy, aren't you, Alexander?'

The wide blue eyes studied her speculatively, almost as if he suspected something of the chaos that was going on in her mind. 'I had another daddy once,' he told her, 'but he went away.'

'I – I know, I'm sorry.' It seemed an inadequate thing to say to console a child for the loss of his father, but she doubted if he remembered him very well for after all he had been only three or four at the time.

'I was a baby then,' he confided with pathetic candour. 'I cried.'

Jane almost cried too, although she told herself she was being ridiculously emotional in the circumstances and her feelings were prompted as much by her own self-pity as by sympathy for the boy.

'You're a big boy now, aren't you?' she said. 'I don't suppose you cry now.'

'Not very often,' he allowed, 'only sometimes I do.'

Jane shook off the depression that threatened to engulf her, determinedly, and smiled at him. 'I'm going along here for a little way,' she told him. 'Shall I talk to you when I come back, Alex? Do they call you Alex?' she added, and he shook his head, although it was obvious he liked the abbreviation.

'No, Mummy doesn't allow it,' he said, then grinned impishly and shrugged his shoulders. 'Sometimes Gavin calls me Alex,' he confided, 'but not when Mummy's there.' Gavin would, Jane thought wryly; he would even take advantage of the woman he was going to marry, and play sly tricks on her with her own son.

'If you like,' Jane told him, 'you can walk along with me as far as the back of your home, will you?'

He nodded, nothing loath, it seemed, and they set off along the edge of the river together. They had gone only a few yards when Jane caught sight of Gavin coming down towards them, one hand raised in greeting, his smile evident when Alexander waved an enthusiastic hand.

So soon after realizing what she had overheard last night and after what the boy had just told her, Jane was reluctant to meet him and she made no effort to return his greeting, but bit hard on her lower lip, feeling the erratic and blinding pulse that hammered away remorselessly at her temple as he strode, long-legged, down the slope.

'I've been looking for you, young man,' he told the boy, an edge of mockery on his grin when he looked at Jane. 'I didn't know you had a girl-friend.'

'She likes throwing pebbles too,' Alexander informed him, with the easy familiarity of children, and Gavin laughed.

'I know,' he said, 'she could never throw straight either.' He rumpled the boy's fair hair and smiled down at him. 'Well, come on, young Alex, we're waiting to go out.'

'Me too?' he asked eagerly, and Jane felt a tug at her heart. It was as if he was sure he would be refused, but still hoped.

'We'll see,' Gavin promised. 'I'll have a word with your mother.' He looked at Jane, a brow arched. 'Are you going back to Pendart?' he asked, and she shook her head, wishing she could think of something appropriate to say that would let him know she knew about

107

him and Ellen Dray.

'No,' she said, 'I'll walk on a bit.'

He studied her for a second and she tried not to colour under his scrutiny. 'Suit yourself,' he told her at last, 'don't get lost.' He took the boy's hand in his and the two of them went off up the slope, the boy running to keep pace with Gavin's long stride.

When Jane eventually got back to Pendart it was not so long before lunch-time and she apologized for being so long. She had even forgotten, she realized with a start, that Peter was due back, and it was only by luck that he had not arrived while she was out.

'It doesn't matter in the least, darling,' Aunt Gaby told her. 'Mr. Frith hasn't arrived yet and there's only two of us for lunch today, Gavin's out.'

'I know,' Jane said. 'I saw him earlier.'

'I rather think he's going somewhere with Ellen Dray,' Aunt Gaby went on, obviously not too pleased at the idea, 'though he was very vague about it as usual.'

'He is going with her, he told me so, though he didn't say it was a lunch date.' Jane looked preoccupied, wondering how much the old lady knew of Gavin's plans. They had always been very close and he usually confided in her, although Jane suspected that the subject of Ellen Dray was one which he would hesitate to mention too often.

'Oh, well, I suppose it's his affair,' Aunt Gaby allowed. 'Did you have a nice walk, dear? But of course you did or you wouldn't have stayed out so long, would you?'

Jane smiled agreement, although it was not entirely true in this instance. 'I find the moor is a good place to think things out,' she told her. 'It's quiet and peaceful and one sees things more in perspective.'

Aunt Gaby's bright, dark eyes were gentle as was the hand that touched Jane's face. 'And you have a lot to think about, haven't you, darling?'

'Quite a bit,' Jane sighed. 'I – I have to find an answer for Peter before too long, and frankly I'm still not positive what to say.'

Aunt Gaby shook her head slowly. 'If you have any doubts at all, Jane dear, please say no.'

Jane laughed ruefully. 'I always have doubts, Aunt Gaby, I'm what they call an indecisive type.' She sighed again, her eyes fixed mistily on the smooth green of the lawn outside. 'But I think I shall marry Peter, Aunt Gaby, I really think I shall.'

CHAPTER SEVEN

PETER'S return to Pendart, far from helping Jane to make up her mind, seemed to make her more indecisive than ever. She accepted his invitation to have dinner in Penford the following night in the hope that when he proposed, as he inevitably would, she would instinctively choose the right answer. It was a vain hope, she realized, but it was the only one she had.

Penford was only a small country town and its restaurants were few, but there was one whose excellent cuisine was well served and its decor old-fashioned. A quiet and discreet place that suited Jane's mood perfectly. It was, unfortunately, one that she had visited often with Gavin in the past, and that added to her pensiveness.

'You look beautiful,' Peter told her as they sat over coffee. 'I've never seen you looking lovelier and I like to think that my being back has something to do with it. It must be true that absence makes the heart grow fonder. I've never believed it before.'

Jane laughed softly, her grey-green eyes almost entirely green in the soft lighting, soft and shining. 'You're really very good for my ego, Peter.' She knew the dress she wore suited her as well as anything she owned and she always felt good in it, even tonight when she was seeking desperately to find the right answer and was less sure than ever now that it came to the point. Her heart pounded alarmingly hard against her ribs as she waited for the inevitable question.

'I'm glad you consider me good for something,' he

declared with a wry smile. It was possible, with the way the tables were arranged, to be almost unobserved by other diners, and Peter took advantage of the conditions to raise her hand to his lips and kiss the palm gently. 'I love you, Jane, and I've missed you horribly while I've been in town.'

'I've missed you too,' she confessed, and laughed softly, without malice. 'It's only three days,' she added teasingly, 'not a lifetime.'

'It seems like a lifetime.' The blue eyes looked much darker in this light and so earnest and sincere that she felt sure she could not refuse him yet again, although she felt a surge of panic at the idea of being committed to anything as serious as an engagement again. The memory of her experience with Gavin still haunted her, though she knew that two years should have been ample time to recover.

'A lifetime is much longer than three days,' she stated, using his own phrase to make her point. 'It's just that, isn't it? For ever and ever, and if it *can't* be happy ever after, then I'd rather it wasn't at all, Peter.'

'It can be,' he urged, one of her hands clasped between both his own, his eyes and the pressure of his fingers intent on persuading her. 'It *can* be happy ever after, Jane, I promise you.'

She lowered her gaze, studying the long, strong hands that held hers. 'But I can't promise *you*, Peter, I wish I could.' She raised her eyes, pleading for understanding. 'I – I'm so – wary, so afraid of doing the wrong thing again as I did before. I couldn't stand to go through that again, Peter, I just couldn't.'

'I know, my darling, I know.' He kissed her fingers gently, his voice as gently soothing as if he sought to console a child. 'I don't blame you in the least, I know how you must feel, but believe me, I won't hurt you, I promise you I won't, and I mean it.'

'Oh, Peter!' There was desperation in her voice as well as pleading and the mist of tears not too far away in her eyes. 'I'm a coward, I know, and it isn't only that I'm afraid of being hurt myself, but that I might hurt you, and I'd hate myself if I did. You've been too sweet and considerate to be played fast and loose with.'

'Try me,' he urged, smiling at her worried face, seeing his goal almost achieved. 'I'm prepared to take a chance on you changing your mind about me, if only you'll say you'll marry me, or at least take the first step and become engaged to me.' He laughed shortly, lifting her chin with one finger so that he could better see her face. 'I'm conceited enough to think you *won't* change your mind about me,' he added.

She shook her head slowly, the tears even closer now. 'If – if you'll agree to keep it just between the two of us for the moment,' she ventured, and saw him frown briefly. 'Just for a little while, Peter,' she pleaded.

He nodded, though she sensed his reluctance. 'I'm bursting to tell the whole world,' he told her, 'but if that's the way you want it, darling, that's the way it shall be, for the moment anyway.' He kissed her fingers fervently, his grip crushing in its strength. 'Just as long as *I* know I don't mind so much who else doesn't.'

His enthusiasm made her smile, although she was already feeling the coldness of doubt in her heart. 'I'll tell Aunt Gaby, of course, I must tell her.'

His expression was mingled doubt and irony as he looked at her. 'It won't be popular with Aunt Gaby,' he declared. 'You realize that, don't you?'

'Aunt Gaby just wants me to be happy,' she told him, speaking slowly and choosing her words carefully.

'It was true what he said, she knew that only too well. Aunt Gaby would be bitterly disappointed, but she would not do or say anything to hurt Jane, she was much too fond of her for that. 'She would rather I – it had been Gavin,' she admitted carefully, 'but she realizes that whatever there was between Gavin and me is finished, and she won't make a fuss about it.'

He was silent for a moment, looking at the hand he held, caressing her fingers with one of his own. 'It *is* finished, isn't it, Jane?' he asked at last, and she nodded, feeling that cold gnawing doubt again and remembering her reaction to the news that Gavin was at last going to marry Ellen Dray.

'Yes,' she said firmly, 'it's finished. He's – he's marrying Ellen Dray.'

Peter looked both startled and curious. 'After all this time?' he queried. 'I wonder why he's waited so long.'

Jane shrugged, suddenly and alarmingly aware that perhaps she herself was the reason. She had made it fairly plain that she would probably marry Peter eventually and, seeing her bent on doing so, he had at last decided to marry Ellen. It was a possibility that gave her little comfort, but she told herself firmly that she would never have gone back to Gavin anyway, it was all over and done with.

She raised her glass, determined not to let Gavin or Ellen Dray intrude again upon her evening. 'Does it matter?' she asked, and he lifted his own glass in a toast to her.

'To us,' he said softly, 'and may we be happy ever after.'

Jane was unusually quiet as they drove home from

Penford, with a light rain flicking like dots of silver in the headlights, the surface of the road already shining wet with it, and Jane sighed for the ride she had planned for tomorrow morning.

Sighing too for the look she would inevitably see in Aunt Gaby's eyes when she told her that she had finally agreed to marry Peter, however tentatively. The old lady had never made any secret of the fact that she wanted nothing more than for Gavin and Jane to marry. It had always been her dream and she had been highly delighted when they had told her they were engaged. This time, Jane thought, she would be much less delighted, but she would not show her disappointment too openly, she felt sure.

They were almost home when a figure loomed darkly in the headlights, making Peter brake hard, cursing softly under his breath. 'What the—!' Jane felt her heart lurch crazily when she recognized Gavin.

His hair clung damply to his head and, as he turned towards them, a smile revealed white teeth against the craggy darkness of his face. Despite the upturned collar of his jacket, he was very wet, though it seemed to bother him very little. He came back towards the car and pushed his head inside when Jane wound down her window, his smile still in evidence. 'Going my way?' he asked.

'Hop in.' Peter's welcome was less than enthusiastic and Gavin pulled a wry face at Jane as he opened the door and climbed in, an intimacy she declined to share. 'Thanks, have you been into the town?'

'We've had dinner in Penford,' Jane supplied reluctantly, wondering why she should suddenly feel so panicky and guilty. It was ridiculous to care what Gavin thought of her being engaged to Peter, but somehow she dreaded the moment when he would inevitably find out.

'The Shade?' he asked casually, almost as if he knew, Jane thought wildly. He did not wait for her to answer but smiled reminiscently. 'Ah, the dinners we've had at that old place, eh, Jane?'

'Yes.' She declined to comment further, aware of Peter stiffly resentful beside her.

Gavin ran his fingers though the thick wetness of his hair, turning down the collar of his jacket. 'Whew! That's better, that fine stuff really soaks through.'

Jane half turned her head, seeking to restore normality to what threatened to develop into a very uncomfortable ride. 'How is it you're on foot?' she asked, and Gavin laughed.

'It was fine when we started out,' he explained, 'and we were using Ellen's car, so I walked to the farm, then of course it started raining.'

'And you had to walk back?' Her tone was comment enough and he laughed again.

'I insisted on walking,' he told her. 'A spot of rain's never hurt me yet and it wasn't worth Ellen turning out again to bring me home.'

'No, of course not.'

There was silence for a moment, both Jane and Peter very conscious of their extra passenger, although he seemed quite unperturbed by the fact that he was probably not welcome.

'Did you have fun in the old town?' he asked, then laughingly answered his own question. 'But of course Penford isn't exactly swinging London, is it, Peter?'

'It's quite a nice old place,' Peter allowed cautiously, and glanced at Jane briefly, with a smile, 'and it's the company that matters most.'

'Oh, every time!' There could have been sarcasm in the reply and Jane turned a brief, suspicious glance on him, only to meet the deep grey eyes head on, their expression both curious and amused. 'It's good for anyone's ego being seen with Jane,' he said.

They turned into the driveway of Pendart, and Peter, with admirable restraint, made no attempt to rise to the obvious bait, but kept silent, if a little tight-lipped as he halted the car in front of the steps. Before he could leave his seat and come round the car, Gavin was out of the back seat and already handing Jane out, a half-smile on his face that she found discomfiting. Peter looked across at him, a hard look of displeasure in his eyes that Jane had seen once before and disliked intensely.

It was a side of Peter she neither knew nor had anticipated, and she wondered how often she would be the cause of that icy look in the blue eyes and the tight hardening of his mouth when he was displeased; it was not a prospect she looked forward to.

Aunt Gaby had already gone to bed when they got in, although Sir Robert was still up and greeted their joint arrival with some surprise. 'I thought you were out together, you and Peter,' he told Jane. 'I didn't know Gavin was along playing gooseberry.'

Jane flushed, more at the look of devilment in Gavin's eyes than his father's choice of phrase. It would be difficult to imagine Gavin in the role of duenna. 'Gavin hasn't been with us, Uncle Robert,' she told him. 'We picked him up along the Penford road.'

'Oh, I see, coming from Dart Farm.' He arched a quizzical brow at his son. 'Did she boot you out into the rain, boy?'

'She did not,' Gavin vowed, undeterred by the suggestion. 'I don't mind walking in the rain at all, but since there was a car available, I cadged a lift, that's all.'

'Hmm.' Sir Robert turned his attention to Jane again, his eyes speculative. 'Gaby seemed to think you were unduly late coming back,' he informed her, 'but I said you'd probably gone to that funny little theatre they've got in Penford.'

'We did, actually,' Jane admitted, suddenly reluctant. 'They were playing—' She cast Gavin a quick, wary look, then shrugged. 'It was an oldie that I hadn't seen done for ages,' she went on, 'and I was curious to see how good the local company are, so Peter indulged me.'

'*Wuthering Heights*,' Gavin said softly, his gaze fixed on her, glittering and dark in the yellow light.

'I said it was an oldie,' she told him, refusing to meet his eyes more than briefly.

'How did the local ham compare?' he asked, while Peter watched them curiously, conscious of some underplay, but uncertain what it was, either forgetting or ignoring the portrait that occupied the dining-room wall so predominantly.

'With what?' Jane deliberately misunderstood him and Gavin laughed, that warm, deep sound she always found so disturbing.

'With the first one you saw,' he told her, challenging her to deny the memory of his own performance, something she could scarcely do with that life-size portrait in the dining-room always there to remind her.

'It was good,' she declared, 'very good. He was well cast and he acted it well.'

'Darling—' Peter began, and she turned bright,

defiant eyes to him that dared him to deny it.

Sir Robert chuckled. 'I can see opinions differ,' he said, 'and if you'll forgive me, I'm in no fit state to listen to the post-mortem, I'm for bed. Jane dear, you could pop in and see Gaby if her light's still on when you come up, would you?'

'I will, Uncle Robert.' She tiptoed and kissed his cheek. 'Goodnight, darling.'

Gavin yawned mightily behind one hand and looked at the two of them with eyes that glittered wickedly. 'I don't want to earn that reputation of gooseberry,' he told them, 'so I'll discreetly withdraw too, and leave you two love-birds in peace.'

'Thanks.' It was Peter being heavily sarcastic, but Jane said nothing, only kept her eyes lowered.

'Goodnight,' Gavin raised a casual hand before making a purely theatrical exit, 'and flights of angels sing thee to thy rest.' The door closed behind him quietly and Jane was left with the feeling that he had deliberately used the quote to remind her of yet another of his earlier roles. It had been his portrayal of Hamlet that had led to his first West End part, and Jane had been there when it happened.

'I won't be too long going up,' she told Peter, suddenly and inexplicably shy at being alone with him, 'in case Aunt Gaby's waiting for me.'

'Why should she be?' He sounded irritated and Jane suspected that he strongly resented the past she had shared with Gavin, not just the time they had been engaged, but the whole exciting wealth of memories from her childhood. No matter how she denied any compatibility now, there would always be those years to bind them inevitably together.

'You heard what Uncle Robert said,' she reminded

him, and smiled, trying to dispel the feeling of exclusion he was suffering from. 'Besides,' she added, 'I can tell her about us.'

He moved closer to put his arms round her, tight and a little hard, his blue eyes earnest and almost pleading. 'I'm not dreaming, am I, Jane? You *did* finally say yes, didn't you?'

'I said a cautious yes,' she admitted, 'if you'll be content with that for the moment.'

'I'm content – for the moment.' He bent his head and kissed her mouth, his lips more demanding than she was prepared for, and she stirred uneasily in his arms. 'Jane!' A frown condemned her protest. 'What's wrong?'

'Nothing's wrong,' she denied. 'I – I suppose I'm just tired, that's all.'

'You're going already?'

'Mm. I want to see Aunt Gaby before she goes to sleep.' She brushed her lips softly over his mouth. 'Goodnight, Peter, I've had a lovely evening.'

He accepted his dismissal with fairly good grace, but there was that tight look about his mouth again that showed his dislike and she almost dubbed it sulky before she realized it was probably his usual response to disappointment. He was apparently less careful about the appearance he presented when he was away from town and more or less relaxed and without his usual business manner.

She turned when they reached her bedroom doorway and he kissed her, gently and without force, holding her close for a long moment, his face against her hair. 'Goodnight, Jane.'

'Goodnight,' she whispered, and glanced across at the strip of light still showing under Aunt Gaby's door.

'I'll go and break the news to Aunt Gaby before she goes to sleep.'

'Goodnight, darling.' He walked along to his own door and turned to wave a hand at her still outside Aunt Gaby's room.

'Jane dear!' Aunt Gaby's dark eyes looked tired, but she still held the book she had been reading, turning it face down when Jane came across and sat on the bed. 'Did you have a good time?'

'I had a very nice time, thank you,' Jane told her with a smile, 'and you should be sleeping, not tiring your eyes with a book at this time of night.'

'I couldn't sleep,' the old lady confessed. 'I don't know why, but I felt restless, and both of you were out. You how how silly I always was when you were both out.'

'We were all three out,' Jane corrected her gently, preparing the way for what she thought might be a difficult moment, and Aunt Gaby nodded acknowledgement of the correction.

'Yes, yes, of course, dear, I forgot for the moment.'

Jane took the small but strong hands in hers and held them gently. 'You mustn't forget any more, darling, not any more.'

The thin fingers stirred under hers and she moved them gently, turning the palms upwards and curling her fingers over them. 'Did you find the answer you wanted?' Aunt Gaby asked, and Jane hesitated only briefly before answering, not meeting the bright, speculative gaze that watched her so closely. She wished she could feel more like a newly-engaged girl should. The almost delirious excitement of the first time, with Gavin, was missing and instead she felt rather sad. It was not at all what she had hoped for and perhaps a little of it showed in her expression, for Aunt Gaby did not look either as surprised or as displeased as Jane expected.

'I found the answer Peter wanted,' she replied, reluctantly honest, 'but – but I've asked him not to make the engagement public knowledge just yet, Aunt Gaby, I – I thought it best.'

'Very wise of you,' Aunt Gaby agreed. 'Have you told Gavin yet?'

Jane frowned, wishing that for once Gavin need not have been brought into the conversation, it did not concern him and she did not see why Aunt Gaby should have expected her to have told him first. 'No,' she said shortly, 'I haven't.'

'I see.'

'Aunt Gaby!' She tried not to sound as exasperated as she felt, but knew she both looked and sounded cross. 'It has absolutely nothing to do with Gavin *what* I do with my life. He's been out tonight with Ellen Dray, he sees her almost every day, *and* her little boy. Alexander told me so, he told me too that Gavin is going to be his new daddy, so I scarcely think Gavin'll have time to spare for me or my affairs. He's far too occupied with his own.' Her tone, she realized, could have been described as petulant and she sounded as if she cared a great deal about what Gavin did even though she denied him interest in her affairs. She should have been more careful, she supposed, especially talking to Aunt Gaby, who was bound to misconstrue her feelings.

'Did the child tell you that?' Aunt Gaby asked, and Jane thought ruefully that it was typical that Gavin, and things concerning him, should take priority.

'He did,' Jane averred, 'when I saw him on the moor yesterday morning, and Gavin came to fetch him. Besides, I—' She bit her lip on betraying the fact that she had overheard that snatch of conversation between Gavin and Ellen Dray, for Aunt Gaby was bound to tell him and it was bad enough having him guess she might have heard them, if he knew for certain he would be unbearable.

'He's said nothing to me.' Aunt Gaby was too pre-occupied to notice the slip, her expression worried as she pondered on Gavin's reticence. Jane, too late, wished she had not been so blunt and told her, but at least it satisfied her own curiosity as to whether the old lady was completely in his confidence or not. Obviously she was not, at least with regard to Ellen Dray.

'I'm sorry, darling.' She squeezed the small hands gently. 'I shouldn't have mentioned it. I should have left it to Gavin to tell you in his own good time.'

'I'm surprised he *hasn't* told me,' Aunt Gaby insisted. 'He's always told me everything, though I must admit he is inclined to be a bit secretive about that young woman.'

'He wasn't very secretive about her where I was concerned,' Jane said wryly. 'He didn't care whether I knew or not that he was seeing her *and* giving her money.' For a moment the old resentment edged her voice and she wondered if it was completely forgotten.

Aunt Gaby sighed deeply. 'I'm afraid she deceived poor Gavin all along the line,' she said. 'He thought he was helping her, but Ellen was never a backward girl and she knew what she was about.'

'So did Gavin,' Jane retorted bitterly. 'He's not a baby, Aunt Gaby, he's a grown man, and if he can't see through her he's a fool and he deserves all he gets.'

'Darling!' The dark eyes looked at her reproachfully. 'You're very hard on him.'

'Hard on him?' Jane looked indignant, her original announcement forgotten in the annoying subject of Gavin. 'He knew quite well that Ellen Dray is an – an octopus, that she had set her heart on having him from the time he was at school, but he *would* treat her like a poor little orphan, no one to turn to, no money – pooh!' Her eyes glistened angrily at the memory of how she had tried to get Gavin to see sense and how he had accused her of being hard and unfeeling. 'Well, if he has no more sense, he deserves all he gets, and I hope he *does* marry her, it serves him right!'

'While you marry Peter?' Aunt Gaby's quiet voice brought her back to reason and she felt a little ashamed of her outburst, although she still rankled under old injustices.

'While I marry Peter,' she agreed. 'At least I know where I stand with Peter, at least he's not likely to go off consoling a baby-faced blonde with the disposition of a – a shark!' She ignored the variety of fishy creatures she had used to describe Ellen Dray, but again felt slightly ashamed of herself for her bitterness.

'I'm sure he won't, dear,' Aunt Gaby said quietly, her eyes glowing with some deep thought that seemed to give her pleasure. 'And I'm sure you'll be very happy. I'd like to wish you every happiness, you and Peter – I'm sorry, I should have said that first, of course. Put it down to tiredness and old age.'

'Tiredness, probably,' Jane allowed, recovering her always volatile temper. She kissed the old lady's forehead gently. 'Old age never!'

'I think I'll sleep now,' Aunt Gaby told her, 'now it's

all settled. Goodnight, dear, I'm glad you and Peter had a nice evening.'

'Goodnight, Aunt Gaby.' She took the book from her and smiled as she put it on the bedside table. 'I'll put this out of the way of temptation!'

It was odd, she thought, as she walked softly to the door, that Aunt Gaby had taken it so well. She had expected more show of emotion, but instead the old lady had seemed to accept it quite calmly.

The bedroom light was off almost before Jane closed the door and she walked softly across the landing to her own door, turning swiftly when another door opened and flooded the landing with light.

She blinked for a moment uncertainly when she saw Gavin outlined against the light, his long length blocking the entire length of the doorway. His room was next to Aunt Gaby's and his sudden appearance, so soon after her leaving, made her uneasy. It was possible he had heard her leave and come out deliberately.

'I thought it was you still prowling about,' he told her, coming across the landing to stand by her so that he need not raise his voice. 'At least I hoped it wasn't your knight errant making midnight visits to his lady-love.'

'Why, you—!' She glared at him angrily, longing to go in and slam the door in his face, but hesitating to make enough noise to rouse the rest of the household, including Peter.

She felt ridiculously weak and trembly as she stood beside him, small and angry. He was wearing the same old white towelling robe she had bought him for his birthday three or four years ago and which always made him look so much darker and disturbingly attractive.

'Sorry.' The apology was superficial and the look in

the grey eyes mocked her anger and the reason for it. 'Have you been having a heart-to-heart with Aunt Gaby?' he asked.

'That's my business!' She opened the door of her room and he immediately defeated her effort to go in and close it on him by putting one hand on the door frame and leaning closer to her, his arm blocking her way.

'Did you have some secret to impart?' he asked, undeterred, and she wondered how much of the conversation he could have heard, for he had very acute hearing, she knew. 'By the way,' he added irrelevantly, 'you look rather fetching in that dress. It suits you, and there's a special shine in your eyes too.'

'I know you can hear through the wall,' she accused him, 'and you've been listening.'

'I can't and I haven't,' he denied blandly. He still kept his voice low, but with difficulty, for it was deep and resonant and meant to carry to the back of a theatre.

'Then how did you—' She stopped when she realized how neatly she had been led on. 'Oh, you're so clever!' she retorted, and he laughed softly, putting a finger to her lips when she raised her voice.

'Instinct,' he whispered. 'I could tell something was in the air when you picked me up along the road, and then when you were closeted with Aunt Gaby, I guessed great things were happening.' Jane said nothing, but stood with her eyes downcast, her gazed fixed on the opening of his robe where the vee exposed several inches of chest, noting irrelevantly that his tan extended at least that far. He studied her for a second or two in silence, then lifted her chin with one finger, so that she instinctively raised her eyes and looked at him.

'Are you happy, Janty?'

'Yes, of course.' She moved her head to evade his hand and the steady gaze he fixed her with.

'Of course,' he echoed softly. 'I hope you mean it, Janty. I'd hate you to do anything without thinking and regret it.'

It was too much for Jane, so soon after recalling the way he had treated her over Ellen Dray, and she lifted her chin defiantly, her eyes sparkling with some other emotion than pure anger. 'I did that once,' she told him, her voice a harsh, desperate whisper. 'I'm more careful now, but this time I'm sure I shan't be made a fool of. Peter loves me.'

'I'm sure he does,' he agreed, 'he'd be a fool not to, but – do you love *him*?'

The question was one she preferred not to be faced with, especially coming from Gavin, and she was all too aware of his eyes on her, waiting and watching. 'Yes – yes, I do.'

'Janty!' The finger lifted her chin again and she knocked his hand away, feeling sheer cold panic when he touched her.

'Don't! Don't touch me, I don't want you to. I love Peter and I'm going to marry him and – and—'

'And you're a very poor liar,' he said softly. He took that vital step nearer and his arms went round her, strong and possessive as his mouth covered hers, stilling the protest she had only half formed. Her heart beat so hard she left sure he must hear it and she felt the weakness in her knees she had always felt at moments like these, then her chaotic thoughts dissolved into something like reason and she remembered it should be Peter who kissed her like that.

'No, Gavin!' She broke free of him and ducked into

her room, closing the door quickly behind her, and leaning against it, trying to still the furious pounding of the blood through her veins, only just hearing the soft whisper of his slippered feet over the landing outside as he went back to his room.

CHAPTER EIGHT

JANE woke next morning with a strangely uneasy feeling, and it was only as she stretched lazily that she remembered the rather tentative promise she had made to Peter last night. One hand went instinctively to her lips a moment later when she remembered, too, the way Gavin had kissed her. It had been a mistake to allow herself to get into such a position where it became inevitable, and she shook her head when she remembered how long it had been before she had made a protest and broken away from him. It did not bear thinking about, what would have happened if Peter had chosen to leave his room too.

The sun shone warmly, filtered through the thin curtains and encouraging her to get up. It was a pretty room and one that had been hers ever since she came to Pendart all those years ago as a rather bewildered little girl, its character changing less than her own had done. She lay for a few moments gazing round her at the comforting familiarity of it. Things changed, people changed, but this room still had a reassuring sameness.

She stretched again and got out of bed, taking her time over bathing and dressing, trying to get used to the idea of being Peter's fiancée, however tentative the arrangement was. She was last down to breakfast, which was unusual, and Sir Robert looked a little surprised at the fact.

He was pouring coffee when she came in and he handed the filled cup to her with a smile. 'Thy need is

128

greater than mine,' he quoted, and Jane took it with a smile of gratitude.

'Thank you, Uncle Robert.'

'Did you sleep well, dear?' Aunt Gaby asked, her eyes noting the slight uneasiness about her that it was impossible to conceal.

'Fine, thank you, Aunt Gaby, I always do here.' She laughed. 'It's all the fresh air, I'm not used to it these days. I'm rapidly becoming a town-bird.'

'Oh, I hope not. You should come home more often,' the old lady urged her. 'Living in London you'll lose your lovely complexion.'

Jane smiled wryly, sipping her coffee and refusing anything to eat as usual. 'I'll survive, darling, millions of us do, and it's where my job is.'

'It's where I am too,' Peter interposed quietly but firmly, before Aunt Gaby could reply, 'and I should object most strongly if I had to travel about two hundred miles every time I wanted to see you.' There was a trace of that stubborn hardness in his eyes when he looked at Jane across the table. 'I want you in town, darling, not buried in the wilds of Exmoor.'

Aunt Gaby looked worried as well as a little surprised at the statement, a slight frown drawing her fine brows together. 'I hope you won't object to Jane coming home to see me sometimes,' she said. 'This *is* her home, Mr. Frith, and she loves the moor. It would be very unkind to prevent her from coming here.'

'Of course it would,' Peter agreed with such an air of gracious concession that Jane frowned over it. 'Of course I wouldn't dream of trying to stop Jane from visiting, Mrs. Drummond, but we do both live and work in town and I consider I have first call on her time, or at least I soon will have.'

Jane could not tell whether he had forgotten his promise to keep their engagement a private matter, or whether he was deliberately letting Gavin know where he stood, but she disliked the way he spoke to Aunt Gaby and the rather autocratic way he was making plans for her.

Gavin, who had said nothing until now, received the statement with mixed feelings, it seemed. There was a glitter of anger behind the amusement in his eyes when he looked across at Peter and the smile crooking his wide mouth was not without malice. Jane watched him uneasily.

'You sound as if you've staked your claim,' he told Peter quietly, and Peter sent Jane a discomfited look that was half apology.

'Perhaps I was talking out of turn,' he admitted reluctantly. He hated making the admission, Jane realized, especially to Gavin.

'Gavin knows about – about us, Peter,' she told him, the consequences of her words unrealized.

For a moment the rather cold blue eyes held hers, half puzzled, half suspicious. 'Does he?' he asked at last. 'May I ask *how* he knows, Jane?'

'I – I told him.' Too late, she realized where the admission had led her and she sought wildly for an escape from her dilemma, conscious of Gavin watching her with a hint of sympathy that didn't help at all.

He said nothing for a moment, stirring sugar slowly into his coffee as if it was a task that required all his attention, then the chill of the blue eyes held her again. 'I left you at Mrs. Drummond's door last night,' he said quietly, 'and, as far as I know, the rest of the household was in bed. There's been no opportunity for the news to have been passed this morning, so how does he know, Jane?'

It was far too much like an inquisition, Jane thought, but nevertheless she sought wildly for an answer that would not involve explaining what had happened after she left Aunt Gaby last night. 'I—' she began, and almost unknowingly sent a look of appeal across the table to Gavin.

'You were wrong on one count anyway,' Gavin told him, his voice soft with an emotion that Jane, from experience, recognized as anger. 'I was still up when Jane left my aunt's room and I spoke to her for a few moments.' Explained like that it sounded all very matter-of-fact, but Gavin was not intent on making a good impression, she realized when she looked at him. 'We talked very quietly so as not to disturb anyone else,' he went on, 'and it didn't seem necessary to have a chaperone present. However, if you think it best, the next time I want to speak to my cousin I'll not only ask your permission but call on you to chaperone us as well.' He got up from the table, tall and seemingly twice as big as usual, his dark face stony with suppressed temper. 'Please excuse me.'

Half a dozen long strides took him to the door and he went out, closing it quietly behind him, while Peter sat, white-faced, his blue eyes glittering and hard, his mouth set tight.

'Peter.' Jane put out a hand instinctively to touch his arm, fearing he might follow Gavin from the room and perhaps become involved in something they would both regret, making *his* position at least irretrievable. It was not beyond Gavin to hit out, she knew, and Peter too looked as if he had violence in mind. The muscles in the arm under her fingers felt hard and tense and she could feel the drumming heaviness of his heartbeat.

'Please, Peter, let it go.'

He made no answer for a moment, but just sat there, taut and angry, while Sir Robert and Aunt Gaby sat in a peculiar, frightening stillness, waiting. Then he laughed suddenly, a short, harsh sound, but relieving them all with the release of tension.

'I'm sorry, I suppose I started that.'

'No,' Jane admitted ruefully, 'I'm afraid I did.' She reached for the coffee pot, smiling apologetically at Aunt Gaby as she did so. 'I'm sorry, darling, I never did stop to think before I spoke, did I? Anyway, it's all out in the open now, isn't it?'

'Do I gather you're going to marry Mr. Frith?' Sir Robert asked, and Jane nodded, warily, wondering how he would take the news. Uncle Robert had always been as keen as his sister to see her married to Gavin and it was possible he would not take kindly to her position with Peter being stabilized at last.

'It's – it's a tentative arrangement at the moment, Uncle Robert,' she explained carefully, 'and we had no intention of telling anyone else yet, but you're family, so you should know really.'

Whether the news pleased or displeased him, he concealed it well and merely extended a polite hand to Peter, who took it rather hesitantly. 'Then I must congratulate you,' he told Peter. 'Jane's a very lovely girl and we're very fond of her. She deserves to be happy and I hope you'll see that she is.' It was a touching little speech and Jane could have taken it at face value had it not been for that last phrase which reminded her irresistibly of Gavin, with its echo of a threat if he did anything to upset her.

'I'll do my very best, Sir Robert.' The promise was solemnly made, and Jane, looking at the serious and earnest face, wondered if she had ever seen that cold, icy anger there such a short time before. Peter seemed to be as volatile in his own way as Gavin was, only in a much more serious way. No expression of Gavin's had ever chilled her as Peter's blue-eyed anger could.

The silence that followed the declaration was tense and full of unspoken questions, and it was left to Aunt Gaby to break into it with something quiet and every-day that could offend no one.

'It's going to be another lovely day,' she said, and Jane smiled at her gratefully.

'I hope so,' she said fervently, her wish not entirely concerned with the weather.

Gavin, she knew, would not long stay out of humour, he never did, and he would probably be back to normal long before lunch time, as annoyingly blithe and uncaring as usual. She was grateful to him for intervening when she so desperately tried to find words to explain to Peter, but she wished he had not been so cross about it or made Peter sound such a suspicious and distrusting man. It was discomfiting to be made to realize that Peter's jealousy would take him to any lengths, and she was not at all sure that Gavin had not deliberately done it to make him show the less at-tractive side of his nature.

As for Gavin losing his own temper, it was a thing that happened so seldom that it only added to her feel-ing of uneasiness.

Peter had brought his riding clothes with him after his visit to London, and Jane quite looked forward to showing him something of the country a bit further afield than they had been so far. They visited the stables and he was well satisfied with the sturdy roan horse Jane suggested he used. She noted with satisfaction that he rode well enough, although he lacked the dash and skill of Gavin's more reckless style.

She would have liked to offer him the grey that Gavin usually rode, but thought it diplomatic not to in view of the friction between them. The animal was quite hard to handle apart from anything else and she would not like to have caused even further bad feeling had the grey played up as he was wont to do. Her own comparison of their respective skills she dismissed impatiently.

'Which way?' Peter asked as they left the yard and headed for the open moor.

Instinctively Jane nodded down the slope in the direction of the distant bulk of Gine Tor and beyond that the dark green coolness of trees.

'It's a favourite haunt of deer in that little bit of forest across there,' she told him. 'You'd like to see them, wouldn't you?'

He turned and smiled at her. 'I just want to go with you,' he admitted, 'I don't mind where it is. If the deer happen to be there too then I'd like to see them.'

She pulled a face over what she considered his lack of enthusiasm, but laughed at his honesty. 'I'm flattered,' she said, 'but I wish you could feel for the country a bit more, as much as I do. Perhaps when you know it better you'll change your mind.'

'Perhaps.' He held the roan with difficulty down the gentle slope, and Jane smiled understanding.

'We'd better let them have their heads for a while,' she suggested, 'they'll perhaps settle down better then; they don't get enough exercise, that's the trouble.'

'Doesn't Sir Robert ever ride?'

Jane nodded. 'When he has the time, which isn't very often, and even when he does, there are three horses to be exercised, so that when neither Gavin nor I are here they don't get out very often anyway.' She saw his hasty frown over the coupling of herself and Gavin and sighed inwardly at the prospect of a future full of such pitfalls to be avoided.

'Let's go!' He put his heels to his mount and was half way down the slope before Jane realized his intent. She touched the mare's hide lightly and urged her after them, sending her bounding over the soft turf willingly in pursuit, exhilarated by the sensation of freedom it always gave her.

'Peter!' She called out to him as she drew nearer. 'That way!' He turned in time to see her pointing finger and waved acknowledgement, taking his mount across the river and towards the distant dark cluster of trees to their left.

They cut across a stream, sending up a scatter of cool silver and on over the open moor, drawing nearer every second to the great grey hulk of Gine Tor. Too late Jane remembered she should have visited the tor again and recovered the shirt she had left there last time she came across this way. Inevitably Peter would be curious about the rocks and might even stop to look at it. It was to be hoped, Jane thought fervently, as they drew ever nearer, that he would not be sufficiently interested to actually go inside, or if he did, that someone had been before them and removed the evidence of her visit.

It was a vain hope that he would not make some comment on the twin points of rock. Joined at their peak and pointing skywards, it drew the eye unfailingly. Already he was reining in the roan to a slower pace and Jane brought the mare alongside her stable-mate, harness jingling as the two heads tossed in satisfaction.

'What's that contraption?' Peter asked, pointing to the tor, now only yards away.

'Gine Tor.' She tried to sound uninterested and would have ridden on, but he had brought his mount to a standstill, eyeing the erection curiously.

'Natural or contrived?' he asked, and Jane laughed.

'Natural, although it doesn't look it; it's rather wonderful, isn't it?'

'Interesting.' He took the roan nearer, peering into the dim interior of the shelter she had shared with Gavin only a few days before. 'Can we look?' He turned inquiringly and she nodded reluctant agreement, following when he dismounted and walked curiously into the arched shelter. 'Hello,' he said suddenly, 'someone else has been here besides us.' He moved towards the pale, crumpled heap that was the shirt he had once insisted on buying for her when she had admired it so in a store window.

Most men she knew would be unlikely to recognize it again, but with Peter she was not at all sure it would be so. He had a neat and tidy mind and also a prodigious memory for detail.

'I shouldn't bother,' she urged, standing just inside the opening, 'someone may come back for it when they miss it.'

It was a vain hope, she realized, as he picked up the now dry silk and looked at it for a moment in silence, a frown growing between his brows. She almost held her breath as he held it up before him in both hands, looking at it closely, then he turned, the frown deepening.

'Expensive tastes your locals have, Jane. This is pure silk and hand-made.' She did not reply, unable to find the right words, and he continued to watch her for a moment. 'It *is* yours, isn't it, Jane?'

She would have denied it, had she thought it would do any good, but it was useless to try and deceive him, so she hoped to make the best of a bad job and laughed lightly as if it had only now occurred to her.

'Oh yes, of course it is, I'd forgotten. I meant to have come back for it, but there's been so much happening it completely slipped my mind.' That at least, she told herself, was the truth. She held out a hand for it, but he shook his head slowly.

'How did it come to be here?' he asked. 'I'd be interested to know. A new and, so you've claimed, favourite garment, and you decide to bring it out on to the moor and lose it, leave it in a – a cave right in the middle of nowhere. You admit I have reason to be curious at least?'

'Yes, of course you have.' She laughed uneasily, feeling the hot colour in her cheeks as she recalled the circumstances in which the shirt had been forgotten. It would be very unwise to tell him the whole truth and yet she saw no alternative. 'It – it was while you were in London,' she told him. 'I came out riding one day and got caught in the most awful storm.'

'So you sheltered in here?' He looked round the dim arched shelter again. 'It's an ideal place, I should think.'

Jane nodded. 'It is – we've often sheltered here before.'

'We?' He was on to the plural so sharply she started almost guiltily, but made no reply. He still held the crumpled silk, suspended from one finger so that it had a sad, dejected look. 'And you found it necessary to – to strip off?'

'I had to!' Jane protested. 'My shirt was soaked through, I hadn't a jacket.' She laughed nervously, finding his manner not only suspicious but intimidating. 'Trust me to come out on a day when it threatened rain, with no jacket!'

'Trust you,' he echoed wryly, eyeing the crumpled shirt. 'You must have been very cold going back,' he added quietly, 'with no jacket and not even a shirt.'

She stared at him for a moment, realizing that there was nothing else to do now but admit that Gavin had been there with her. 'I—' she began, but he threw the bundle of silk at her before he strode out of the rock and past her to where the horses were standing.

'Don't bother, Jane, I can guess the rest.'

'Peter!' She was only a step behind him as he strode across the turf. 'Peter, please!'

He turned, the icy hardness in his blue eyes again, his mouth set firm against her explanation. 'You don't have to explain anything to me, Jane,' he told her. 'I may be a fool, but I can see far enough to put Gavin Blair firmly behind that little episode. I'm only sorry you saw fit to fall in with his plans.'

'But I didn't!' She would never have pleaded so earnestly if she had stopped to think how unfair he was being, but she was only concerned at the moment with making him see the truth. 'Please, Peter, listen to me!'

The plea was irresistible as she was sure it would be and his expression was already less antagonistic when he looked down at her, then he put his hands to hold her by her shoulders, shaking his head slowly. 'It *was* Gavin you were with,' he told her, in a tone that refused to believe anything else.

'Yes, it was,' she admitted, 'but it wasn't as you seem to think.'

'Do you *know* what I think?' he asked.

'I – I can guess.' She was stung into being defensive at last, but raised her eyes appealingly. 'I came out alone, I felt like being alone. It came on to rain and before I knew where I was it was pouring down in the most awful storm, so I headed for here, for Gine Tor, as I said, we – I've often sheltered here in the past and it was instinctive, I suppose. Gavin came along from out of nowhere. I didn't even know he was out, but he must have been coming along behind me and I didn't notice him. I couldn't very well refuse to share my shelter with him in a storm like that, it wouldn't have been reasonable.'

He glanced back at the small, intimate shelter the rock offered, his eyes dark with all manner of possibilities. 'Very cosy,' he said wryly, 'but it doesn't explain the shirt, does it?'

'I told you it was wringing wet,' Jane protested. 'It was stupid to keep it on when it was so wet, and Gavin loaned me his jacket, it's as simple as that.'

He shook his head again, a determined glint in his eyes, refusing to be mollified by so simple an explanation. 'Nothing's simple where you and Gavin Blair are concerned,' he declared. 'Can't you see what he's up to, Jane? Can't you?'

'He's going to marry Ellen Dray,' Jane said, and wished she could have sounded more pleased about it, 'so I can't think he's so intent on pursuing me.'

'Oh, for heaven's sake, darling, he's a man who's used to having his cake and eating it too, *and* he intends to go on doing so, can't you see that?'

Jane shook her head, horribly uncertain. 'I—' she

began, but an impatient hand cut her short.

'He'll never give up, Jane, he'll keep on until he gets you back, then he'll do as he did before – make a fool of you with Ellen Dray, whether he marries her or not.'

'No, he *won't*,' Jane denied crossly, 'because I shan't *go* back to him – not that I believe for one minute that he wants it that way, he's quite happy with things as they are, it seems to me.'

'I wish to heaven he *would* marry Ellen Dray,' Peter told her shortly, 'and you'd marry me, then there'd be an end to all this.'

Jane laughed, a laugh without humour, her gaze downcast so that he should not see the look in her eyes. 'He *is* going to marry her,' she declared, 'but if Gavin makes up his mind, marriage isn't going to make any difference.'

Much as she usually enjoyed his company, Jane felt she needed time by herself to think things out, time to decide once and for all just what it was she wanted to do. Being engaged to Peter had solved nothing for her as far as being sure of herself was concerned, for she was as unconvinced as ever that Peter was exactly the right man for her, and yet the alternative was to have to face Gavin's I-told-you-so smugness when she broke the engagement. Not to mention the hopeful eyes of Aunt Gaby as she speculated on the real reason behind her decision.

She pleaded a headache a day or so later when Peter suggested that she accompany him to Exeter to see an uncle he had not seen for years.

'I haven't seen him for ages,' Peter told her after lunch, 'and I can't very well be in the area and not visit him. Are you sure you won't come with me, Jane?'

'I don't think so, thank you,' she smiled. 'I really do have a headache and I wouldn't be very good company at all – besides, if you take me along your uncle may jump to conclusions and then before we know where we are our – our arrangement will be public knowledge in no time.'

'Frankly I don't care if it is,' he declared a little impatiently. 'The sooner the better as far as I'm concerned. Anyway,' he added, 'you've told your family, so I don't quite see why mine shouldn't be just as privileged.'

'Yes, yes, I'm sorry, Peter.' She tiptoed and kissed him lightly beside his mouth. 'I'm a selfish, quarrelsome little horror and I wonder you still want to be bothered with me,' she told him, pulling a face.

'You know why,' he said, his voice low and not quite steady, then he pulled her into his arms and kissed her, firmly and determinedly until she was breathless and protesting. 'You're beautiful and adorable and I love you to distraction,' he told her, 'and the sooner you marry me the happier I'll be.'

Jane laughed softly, her eyes big and shinily green as she looked up at him. 'You're very convincing,' she told him, 'but don't rush me, Peter.'

'I'm not rushing you,' he denied, and kissed her throat, 'but I love you so much, my darling Jane, so don't keep me waiting too long, please. In the meantime I shall tell my Uncle Ted that I'm engaged to the most beautiful girl in the world.'

'And probably the most unreliable,' she warned him.

'Nonsense!' He kissed her again lightly on her forehead. 'Are you sure you won't come with me, darling?'

She shook her head, smiling. 'No, Peter, I'd really rather not. You can talk family affairs and I'll go and sit by the Medd and meditate, I think, I've so much to think about.'

'Alone?' The edge of suspicion on his voice spoiled the moment for her and she frowned.

'Of course alone,' she declared, and raised her eyes to him steadily. 'Don't you trust me?'

'I trust *you*,' he told her bluntly. 'It's Gavin Blair I don't trust.'

'Well, he's almost sure to be seeing Ellen Dray,' Jane retorted, 'so you needn't worry anyway.'

It was, Jane decided shortly afterwards when she saw him off to Exeter, going to be an uphill fight to convince Peter that it was finally and absolutely finished with her and Gavin.

CHAPTER NINE

It was tranquil and sunny and blessedly quiet in the big room and, with Peter away, Jane felt herself more able to relax. She had found herself a book, delaying her walk by the river until later in the afternoon and she sat, half drowsily, in one of the armchairs, her attention barely held by the book. Her thoughts frequently returning to the increasingly urgent problem of Peter.

Aunt Gaby was visiting an old friend in Penford and Sir Robert was, as usual, working so that she had the house to herself except for Mary, the housekeeper, and for once she was not averse to her own company.

She had not been peacefully alone for more than half an hour, however, when the door opened to admit Gavin, his brows raised at the sight of her solitude. He was the last person she had expected to see or hoped to see, and she frowned.

He glanced, with exaggerated care, round the room, presumably in search of Peter and, failing to see him, looked at her wide-eyed. 'Have you been abandoned? he asked, ignoring her discouraging frown. 'Where's your faithful swain?'

'If you mean Peter,' she told him, stiffly unfriendly, 'he's visiting an uncle in Exeter.'

She looked down at her book again, hoping he would take her abruptness for dismissal, or at least that he would sit down quietly and leave her in peace, but it was a vain hope with Gavin.

'You haven't another faithful swain in these parts,

have you?' he grinned. 'Except me, of course.'

The statement was so blatantly provocative that she glared at him, but refused to be drawn into one of their interminable arguments – the arguments that always seemed to end with her losing her temper and Gavin looking wickedly pleased with himself for having scored off her.

'Are you going to maintain an icy silence?' he asked, dropping into one of the armchairs.

Jane sighed deeply in sympathy with herself and put her book down on the arm of her chair with studied care. 'I had hoped,' she told him, as if her patience was sorely tried with having to explain to him, 'to be able to read quietly in here, for a while at least, but if you insist on talking I can always go upstairs to my room.'

'You unsociable little devil,' he declared, laughing at her indignant expression. 'Are you sulking because Peter's gone off and left you, or is it that you're particularly averse to *my* company?'

'Peter hasn't gone off and left me,' she denied. 'I could have gone with him had I wanted to, but I preferred to stay and be quiet. I'm not in the mood for company.'

'So you're feeling unsociable,' he said, finding the fact amusing judging by his smile. 'Snap out of it, Janty, you used not to be such a little misery. What's happened to you lately?'

'*You* have!' Jane retorted. 'I was perfectly happy when I arrived here and prepared to enjoy a holiday with Peter, then you had to turn up and spoil everything!'

'I'm sorry.' His hurt, she was startled to realize, was genuine and she felt the colour warm her cheeks, as she fought with the desire to tell him she did not mean it.

'Did you know I was here before you came?' she asked. It was a question she had wanted to ask often before but had always hesitated over, and she saw him smile with his more usual self-confidence.

'Of course,' he told her. 'I thought two years was long enough for anybody to sulk. I thought you might be prepared to bury the hatchet.'

'I – I was.' She dared not look at him, remembering how much he had been in her thoughts all the way down from London and how often she had mentally strayed from Peter as they drove along the moor-edged roads to Pendart.

'I didn't realize how serious you were with Peter Frith,' he admitted. 'I knew he was mad about you, that's not difficult, heaven knows, but I didn't realize you were on the verge of marrying him.' She could almost see him shrug off the serious mood he had fallen into, and saw the inevitable smile widen his mouth. 'When *is* the happy day?' he asked. 'Have you fixed it yet?'

'Have you?' She could not resist the retort and saw him blink for a moment, uncertainly.

'Have I what?' he asked quietly, and she traced the pattern on the cover of her book with one finger, not looking at him and not really wanting to know the answer.

'Fixed a wedding date with – with Ellen?'

'No.' He still looked and sounded wary.

'Then why should I be in any more of a hurry to marry Peter? After all, you and Ellen Dray have been together far longer than Peter and me.'

His smile had the old rakish curl to it and his eyes teased her, though gently. 'Together sounds most immoral,' he told her. 'And Ellen, no matter what you think, darling, is still a respectable young widow.'

'I – I didn't mean it like that, Gavin!' She looked up then and saw that she had been drawn yet again into a position where she was in the wrong. 'Oh, you – you just have to make me look small, don't you?' She got up from her chair, closing the book with an angry bang, and glaring down at him as he sat, confidently at ease, in the depth of an armchair.

'You are small,' he grinned, deliberately misunderstanding her. 'Five feet two isn't exactly giant, darling.'

'Don't darling me!' She was thoroughly angry now and longed to be able to win an argument, just once. 'Save it for Ellen.'

'You're still jealous of her, aren't you?' He eyed her speculatively, unworried by the ominous gleam in her eyes. 'I should think Peter would find your reaction rather off-putting.'

'Peter loves me,' she told him. 'He understands me and knows why I – I dislike Ellen. I'm certainly not jealous of her, I never was, not in the usual sense of the word. I was just so furious because you couldn't see through her. I thought you had more intelligence than to be caught by *that* old story, but—' she sighed as if she found it unbelievable still – 'you swallowed it hook, line and sinker.'

She saw the grey eyes narrow for a moment and look darker suddenly, and recognized the signs of his rare temper. At last, she thought, she had put him in a position that he could not talk his way out of. He could not deny that Ellen Dray had fooled him and he did not like being reminded of it. She should have felt pleased with herself, but in fact she only felt rather sorry that she had been so blunt. Gavin too, like most people who are slow to anger, had a furious temper when it was roused and she was a little apprehensive at being on the receiving end of it.

'At last we have it,' he said quietly, too quietly. 'You think I was taken in by a hard-luck story that had no truth in it. Well, you're wrong, Jane. You were wrong two years ago and you're still wrong. Ellen *did* need help, and if it happened again I'd do exactly the same thing again whether you stormed off in a tantrum or not.'

She recognized the stubborn, unyielding set of his jaw and knew he would never admit to being fooled, even if he knew it, and she was certain he did not. 'I acted in the only way I could,' she said defensively. 'No woman can be expected to stand by and watch her — her fiancé behave as you did with Ellen.'

A trace of his old bravado showed for a moment in his eyes and he half-smiled. 'I've said it before, Janty, and I'll say it again, you've been spoiled silly and you just never learned to see anybody else's side of a question. Maybe Peter will handle you a little more firmly than I did. I was too soft, I helped to spoil you when you were a tiddler, I suppose, that's why I let you go off instead of turning you over my knee and spanking some sense into you.'

'Oh, you—!' She stood staring at him helplessly for a moment, still deterred by the darkness of temper in his eyes, then without another word, she dropped the book she had been holding into the armchair and went out of the room, her knees trembling weakly and a prickle of tears in her eyes.

Almost without thinking she left the house and headed for the clean, open expanse of the moor, her hands clenched at her sides, the hot flush of anger still in her cheeks as she started down the green slope towards the sparkling lure of the tiny river.

It was almost instinctive to come out here when she needed to think or to throw off some mood that troubled her and she felt herself begin to relax before she had gone more than halfway down the incline. There was no better place to be at a time like this than her beloved moor.

It was a warm, bright day and a lark soared into the sky, hovering above its well-concealed nest, its sweet, flute-like song hanging in the summer air and cascading like tiny bells over the vastness of the moor. The turf smelled tangy and with the sweeter, spicier smell of the heather and bracken, made the fragrance that Jane would have known, even in blindness.

The river was higher since the heavy storm a few days ago, but it was still quite shallow and clear as crystal as it ran over its stony bed. Walking beside it reminded Jane of the little boy, Alexander, whom she had met here, and who had given her so much to think about. He had been so certain that Gavin was to be his stepfather and, with the conversation she had overheard between Gavin and Ellen Dray, Jane had no difficulty believing it. It was only Gavin's own reticence in the matter that puzzled her. He had not been drawn by her question about a wedding date and had almost pointedly evaded the subject.

She sighed as she sat down on the river bank, hugging her knees to her and gazing into the clear, crystal coolness of the water. Once it had been impossible to be anything but happy here on the moor, now, although she had shed some of her despondency, she still felt low and far more dispirited than she would once have thought possible.

She wondered if Aunt Gaby had said anything to Gavin about his own plans to marry Ellen Dray, and thinking of that, she frowned. She should not have told Aunt Gaby about that, she should have left it to Gavin to tell her himself in his own good time. None of them, herself included, could claim to be surprised at the news, only that it had taken so long to happen. Two years, she thought bitterly, should have been ample time for a woman like Ellen Dray to bring a man round to her ideas, especially when he spent so much time with her.

As to Peter – she sighed again, resting her chin on her knees; she had crossed that bridge now and there was nothing for it but to face the fact that she would eventually marry him. He had the right to expect it now, even though her answer had been wary and the agreement tentative. There was a limit to any man's patience and Peter, she thought, was rapidly approaching his.

She had sat there for some time when different sounds intruded into her consciousness. After a second or two, while she identified the sound of a horse's progress, she turned round, frowning slightly over the prospect of having her solitude disturbed.

A white and brown skewbald mare picked its way daintily over the heather, its shoes striking flintily on the occasional pebble, and Jane's frown deepened when she recognized the rider. Ellen Dray sat straight and rather arrogant in the saddle, her cold blue gaze noting Jane sitting at the water's edge.

Jane, unsure how long she had been out there, looked for Gavin to see if he had gone out after she left, but there was no sign of him, so presumably he had declined to join her this time.

The baby-blue eyes narrowed against the sun and a

wide-brimmed hat shaded her pale skin from over-exposure. Combined with white trousers and a pale yellow shirt, she looked somehow foreign, and quite unlike the more formal English rider, so that Jane was reminded of Aunt Gaby's disapproval on the first day she arrived home. Such a costume would almost certainly have been frowned on by Aunt Gaby, although Jane had to admit that the blonde girl looked quite attractive in it.

The mare was reined in and fine brows arched curiously. 'All alone, Jane?'

Jane nodded, feeling rather vulnerable from her seat on the ground with the other girl so high above her. 'For the moment,' she agreed. 'Are you?'

'For the moment.' The full mouth curved into a smile that looked far more friendly than the expression in her eyes. 'You look rather forlorn crouched down there. You haven't quarrelled with your – your friend, have you?'

Jane flushed as she shook her head, getting to her feet so as to dispel that vulnerable feeling. 'No, I haven't quarrelled with Peter,' she said. 'He's visiting a relative in Exeter.'

The brows rose again. 'Without you?'

'Without me,' Jane echoed. 'I wasn't feeling very much like visiting and they'll have a lot to talk about after so long.'

'Is he going to break the good news to – whoever it is?'

'Possibly,' Jane conceded, disliking the way she was being questioned.

'When's the big day to be?' Ellen pressed on, ignoring Jane's obvious dislike. 'You *are* getting married, aren't you?'

Jane hesitated, looking at the fair, doll-like face for a moment thoughtfully. 'I presume Gavin told you about my being engaged to Peter,' she said at last, watching for her reaction.

'Yes, as a matter of fact he did.'

Jane tightened her mouth on the knowledge. 'I thought he would. Well, it's true I have become tentatively engaged to Peter, but the news was supposed to have been only known to the family, not made general knowledge, and I have no idea *when* the big day's to be, I'm sorry.'

The apology was deliberately sarcastic and she saw Ellen's eyes narrow maliciously. 'Oh, you must have some idea, surely,' she told her. 'There's no point in being secretive, is there?'

'None at all,' Jane agreed, 'but for one thing – I really don't know when it will be, and quite frankly, Ellen, I can't see that it should concern you even if I did.'

Anger sparkled in the narrowed eyes and the smile had a tight, set look that reminded Jane uneasily of Peter. 'Oh, please forgive my curiosity,' Ellen begged harshly, 'but I *do* have a rather personal interest in it, you know. The sooner you're married to your Peter, the better I'll be pleased, then Gavin can stop worrying about you.'

'*Does* he worry about me?' Jane asked, plainly interested. 'I can't think why.'

'Because he has an exaggerated sense of guilt about you,' she was told. 'He feels he may have put you off marriage by breaking that silly engagement two years ago. I keep trying to make him see that it would never have worked out, but—' She shrugged, her smile mocking. 'You know Gavin.'

'I thought I did.' Jane held her temper with difficulty in the face of such derogatory reference to her broken engagement. Apart from the fact that it had been she and not Gavin who had broken it off, there had been nothing silly about it at all. It was something she did not intend discussing with Ellen Dray, however.

'Well, I think I can claim to know him *very* well,' Ellen assured her, 'and he's as anxious to see you married and settled as I am.'

'I'm touched by your concern.' Jane tried not to let her voice quaver. 'However, I've no intention of rushing into marriage to suit either you or Gavin.'

'I see.' The icy look in the blue eyes made Jane shiver and she would have turned and walked away, further along the bank, anywhere away from that cold, malicious gaze, but the handle of a riding crop touched her shoulder and she turned back, startled. 'If you're going to marry your Peter, then marry him,' Ellen Dray told her harshly. 'I want you as far away as possible from here. I want you out of Gavin's life for good, Jane Drummond, and I'll stop at nothing to see you go. Away from Pendart, back to London, anywhere out of Gavin's way.'

For a moment Jane stared at her, appalled by the malice directed at her, but strangely roused by the other girl's anxiety that she should not see Gavin again. Perhaps Ellen Dray was not as sure of him as she would obviously like to be. 'Pendart is my home,' she said slowly. 'I shall always come back here sometimes, even if I do marry Peter.'

'*If* you do?' The harsh voice grated on Jane's nerves.

'If I do,' Jane repeated. 'Nothing is certain until it

happens, Ellen, and as I say, I shall still be coming home.'

The information was received in cold-eyed silence for a moment. 'Then I'll have to make sure we aren't here at the same time,' Ellen told her chillingly, and Jane shrank from the possessive 'we'.

For the first time she noticed Ellen's long, thin hands, in fact it looked almost as if she was intent on drawing attention to them. Curled round the reins, holding the restless mare in check, she used them far more flamboyantly than was necessary, and then Jane suddenly realized the reason for it.

It was almost impossible not to notice the large and rather opulent-looking opal that adorned her left hand and glowed richly in the sunlight.

'You like it?' she asked, smiling satisfaction and spreading her hand the better to show the ring, and Jane nodded silently. 'I adore opals, don't you?'

'They're – they're very beautiful,' Jane agreed, remembering her own lovely sapphire and diamond ring.

She felt very small and vulnerable suddenly and in need of Peter's comforting arm, and she turned away once again from the icy malice in Ellen Dray's eyes, anxious to be gone. Before she could take even one step, however, the mare was urged into action and the heavy body caught Jane on one shoulder and sent her toppling backwards into the river behind her, ducking her completely.

She was unsure whether she made any sound or not, but she was suddenly and horribly conscious of the coldness of water enveloping her, making her gasp and splutter. It was several moments before she shook the water from her face and head sufficiently to be aware of the sound of distant, harsh laughter and the disappearing drum of hooves over the turf and heather as Ellen Dray rode off.

Too stunned for a while by the suddenness of it, Jane simply sat there in the water, staring down at the cloudy brownness that swirled round her, where the soil had been disturbed by her fall.

Carefully she began to get to her feet, shaking off the worst of the water from her hair and her hands, clumsy in the swift flow, as she tried to wring out the clinging wetness of her dress. Ellen Dray was rapidly disappearing into the distance without even a backward glance, and tears of anger and frustration blurred Jane's vision as she stared after her.

It was other laughter, deep, warm laughter this time, that made her spin round, her eyes blazing anger through her tears, knowing who her tormentor was even before she saw Gavin. She clenched her fists, blindly furious that he should have come along at just the right time to witness her humiliation.

'Stop laughing!' she stormed at him. 'Stop laughing and go away!'

'I've heard of cooling off,' he told her, surveying her from the bank, 'but this is ridiculous.'

'Go away and leave me alone!' She wanted to see him less than anyone at the moment and she was horribly afraid of crying and making a fool of herself in front of him.

'I know you needed to cool down after our little fracas earlier,' he went on, 'but couldn't you have found some more conventional way of doing it?'

It was typical of him, she thought crossly, to have recovered his own good humour so quickly and expect her to have done the same, but he could not know that she had seen Ellen Dray and been dazzled by that blazing opal.

He could have told her, she thought, that the girl was wearing his ring, especially since they had been discussing his relationship with her. It was sly and secretive and quite unlike him, she had to admit, not to have mentioned it. Or perhaps the Gavin she had known no longer existed, an idea she faced unwillingly.

'Go away,' she repeated. 'I'm not in the mood for your jokes, Gavin.'

'I *was* going to haul you out,' he told her, his eyes showing both amusement and sympathy, 'but of course if you *like* total immersion with all your clothes on, then don't let me deter you.'

She started to walk out of the shallow water, refusing the hand he proffered, her shoes slipping and sliding on the smooth pebbles, and she would have fallen again if he had not come to her aid and lifted her out bodily, carrying her on to the bank, laughing at her wildly indignant protests.

'Let me go!' she yelled at him furiously. 'Let me *go*!'

'All right, all right.' He dumped her unceremoniously on to the grass and stood looking down at her, quite undisturbed by her anger. 'What happened to you, anyway?'

Tears still blurred her vision and she choked on her words, brushing a wet hand across her eyes to clear them. 'You wouldn't believe me if I told you.'

'Try me.' He glanced over his shoulder at the rapidly disappearing figure on the skewbald, still easily recognizable as Ellen Dray, and there was speculation in the grey eyes.

He would certainly never take her word against Ellen's in the circumstances. 'I – I fell in, isn't that good enough for you?' she asked. 'And I'm horribly wet and my hair's ruined.'

'Oh, you *are* a little Moaning Maggie, aren't you?' he laughed. 'Come on, let's get you home and dried out.' He took off his jacket and put it round her shoulders. 'You seem to spend more time in my jacket than I do.'

'I don't *want* your jacket.' She shrugged out of it and started to walk away from him, her shoes squelching wetly at every step. 'Ugh! It's horrible!'

'Don't be pig-headed, Janty.' He recovered the jacket and replaced it round her shoulders, then, before she realized his intent, he had swept her up into his arms and was striding up the slope with her, as if she weighed no more than a child.

It was the final humiliation and she felt the tears rolling warmly down her cheeks as she instinctively put one arm round his neck and held on tight. 'Put me down,' she told him, 'Gavin, put me *down*!'

Even while she was protesting so vigorously, her mind was busy with the prospect of what would happen if Ellen Dray chose that particular moment to ride back that way, and she had to admit to wishing she would. That huge opal flashed tauntingly into her mind's eye again and she turned her head to glare at him indignantly, but found the grey eyes disturbingly close, the laughter in them doing nothing to appease her.

'Put me down!' she repeated, hating the way her colour rose under his scrutiny.

'I'll dump you back in the river if you don't stop behaving like a spoiled five-year-old,' he threatened.

'And if you have such a rooted objection to me carrying you, why are you hanging on so tight?'

'I'm – I'm not.' She tried to withdraw her arm from round his neck, but her position made it impossible and he laughed.

'Poor Janty, you can't win, can you, darling?' She did not answer, but kept her eyes studiously averted. 'Talking of the river,' he added, 'how *did* you manage to get in there in the first place?'

'I told you, I fell in,' she insisted stubbornly.

'And I don't believe you. You're far too used to these rivers to just fall in.'

She thought for a moment or two. 'Suppose I told you I was pushed in deliberately,' she ventured, curious to see his reaction, 'would you believe me?'

He studied her for a moment, thoughtfully. 'I just might,' he said cautiously. 'Tell me.'

'You saw Ellen Dray leaving,' she told him, 'you must have done.'

The steady gaze did not waver, but his eyes narrowed very slightly and there was an unfamiliar tightness about his wide, straight mouth that looked ominous. 'I saw Ellen riding away,' he agreed quietly, evidently bent on making her tell the whole story instead of guessing for himself.

'Well, now you know the answer,' Jane told him.

'Are you telling me that Ellen pushed you into the river, deliberately?'

'She put her heels to the mare and rode straight at me,' Jane told him, 'and the mare's weight sent me flying. I call that pushing me in.' She looked at him with a glint of defiance behind the tears. 'Now I suppose you'll say you don't believe me again,' she added before he could speak. 'You don't think your – your lady friend is capable of doing such a thing. Well, go ahead and say it. I don't care, it's perfectly true no matter what you think.'

'I think Ellen's perfectly capable of dunking you in the river,' he allowed mildly. 'As capable as you would be in her place.'

Jane stared at him, round-eyed. 'I—' she began, and he laughed shortly.

'Don't look so wide-eyed and innocent, darling. You pushed me in the river umpteen times when you were a little'un and I don't imagine you've grown up any more virtuous than the rest of us, especially in that direction.'

'Thank you.' She held herself as stiffly as she was able in the circumstances and he laughed again at her indignation, taking the last few feet of the slope in his stride.

He strode across to the garden gate and pushed it open with one foot, then, suddenly and surprisingly as he stood there under the lilac that guarded the gate, he bent his head and kissed her gently on her mouth. 'Poor Janty,' he said softly.

CHAPTER TEN

Aunt Gaby clucked sympathetically over Jane's bedraggled appearance, for she had just returned from her visit when Gavin came in through the rear door of the house carrying Jane, and dumped her squelchily on to her feet in the hall.

'Whatever happened, dear?' Aunt Gaby asked.

'I fell in the river.' Jane was not prepared to go into details, especially while she was still wet through and thoroughly miserable about it. She was feeling oddly weepy too, more so since Gavin had kissed her so gently out there in the garden. Now that he was really engaged to Ellen Dray the least he could do was to behave as if he was.

If Jane was unwilling to explain her dilemma, however, Gavin had no such qualms. He gave Aunt Gaby a wink that conveyed far more than words and smiled meaningly. 'She met a horse in a hurry,' he told her, 'and lost the fight.'

Aunt Gaby frowned. 'Darling, that doesn't make sense.'

'It doesn't,' Gavin agreed amiably, 'but Jane claims that Ellen rode at her and knocked her into the river.'

His tone left room for doubt and Jane glared at him, her wet hair dripping dismally on to her shoulders so that she tossed it back impatiently. 'She *did* ride at me deliberately,' she insisted, 'though I don't expect you to believe me in the circumstances.'

'I didn't say I didn't believe you,' he denied, 'and I

don't know what circumstances it is you keep referring to.'

'That you're – oh, you're just being difficult, Gavin!' She refused to go into his relationship with Ellen here and now. He could scarcely expect her to congratulate him and it was not her place to break it to Aunt Gaby. She looked down at the wet patches on the hall floor where her wet shoes had seeped, and made a grimace of apology at Aunt Gaby. 'I'm sorry I've made such a mess, Aunt Gaby, but I couldn't help it.'

'Of course you couldn't, darling,' Aunt Gaby consoled her, 'but you'd better go and get out of those wet clothes as soon as you can, and have a hot bath too, that's always a help when you've had a ducking.'

Jane did not argue, but turned and went upstairs, aware that Gavin was watching her with an expression that was as much puzzled as amused, and once more she felt horribly close to tears, though she told herself she was a fool for feeling like that.

She took her time bathing and changing and by dinner time only a lingering dampness in her hair betrayed her ducking, and that could easily be explained by getting it wet in her bath.

She had no intention of saying anything to Peter about her falling foul of Ellen Dray, for he would only make a fuss and, worse, probably pick a quarrel with Gavin about it if he knew about his subsequent rescue. It was something she had no qualms about keeping from him and she let Aunt Gaby know her reasons. Gavin, she hoped, would realize silence was *his* best policy too.

'It's the annual summer dance next week,' Aunt Gaby announced at dinner. 'You remember the Penford Ladies' Club, Jane? Margaret Hannon's this year's secretary and she asked me if you and Gavin would be coming as you were both here.' The bright dark eyes flicked from Jane to Gavin and back again. 'I *did* explain, of course,' she added.

'*Did* you?' Gavin eyed her wickedly. 'How clever of you, love.'

Aunt Gaby did no more than make a moue of reproach at him. 'Margaret said to ask you both anyway, you could each bring your own partners.'

Gavin made no further comment, but merely looked rather maliciously amused, so it was left to Jane to answer and she looked across at Peter, smiling hopefully. 'You'll come, won't you, Peter?' she asked. 'It's only a small place and everyone's very nice, we all know each other, and I'm sure you'd enjoy it.'

'Of course, darling, if you'd like to. You know I'll come if you want me to.'

Jane frowned, wishing Peter would show some enthusiasm for something for its own sake and not always sound as if he was merely doing it to oblige her. It was a habit that was beginning to irritate her and she thought Gavin at least recognized it, for her caught her eye and made a grimace that was both sympathetic and amused.

'I don't want to drag you off to a dance if you're going to be bored,' Jane told Peter shortly, partly because Gavin's expression annoyed her.

Peter looked a little surprised for a second, then he shook his head. 'I shan't be bored at all, Jane, I quite like dancing sometimes, though I'm horribly out of practice.'

'Not much scope for the romantic waltz in the boardroom,' Gavin sympathized. 'I often think big business must be a bit like a monastery, not many opportunities for letting your hair down.'

Peter looked at him for a moment, his expression disapproving. Business to Peter was never a subject for levity. 'Most of us manage to do very well,' he said, glancing at Jane meaningly, and she hastily lowered her eyes.

'Gavin, what about you, darling?' Aunt Gaby asked. 'Will you be going?'

Jane was uncertain what she hoped his answer would be, but Aunt Gaby, she thought, was definitely anxious. 'Of course, my love.' He smiled widely as if he too suspected something behind her question, and Aunt Gaby sighed her relief audibly.

'I'm afraid I've been rather naughty,' Aunt Gaby confessed, smiling at him hopefully.

Gavin eyed her suspiciously for a second. 'Go on,' he urged her, 'tell me the worst, darling. What have you let me in for?'

'It's nothing very terrible,' Aunt Gaby assured him. 'I said – I more or less promised you'd be a prize, that's all.'

Gavin stared at her. 'A prize? What kind of a prize, for heaven's sake? You make me sound like a box of chocolates or a brass tray at a fair!' Jane could not resist a giggle and he looked at her reproachfully.

'They have draw prizes, Gavin, you remember. They charge quite a lot for the tickets and the prizes are very good.'

'I agree wholeheartedly in this case,' Gavin said fervently. 'What exactly does being a prize involve? Do I merely have to dance with the lucky lady, or am I committed for life?'

'Of course not.' Aunt Gaby shook her head. 'The lady who wins is entitled to an evening out with you in

Exeter. The girls will be thrilled to bits,' she added. 'You're a much bigger attraction than Mr. Bail, the local dancing champion – he was last year's prize.'

'Did he survive the ordeal?'

'Yes, of course. Gavin, do be serious.' She looked at him anxiously for a moment. 'You will do it, won't you, Gavin?'

'I won't pretend the idea thrills me,' Gavin admitted, 'but since you've pledged your immortal soul on it, Aunt Gaby, I'll do it.'

'Thank you, darling, I'll let Margaret Hannon know first thing in the morning.'

'You're a cunning old lady,' Gavin told her with a grin. 'You knew I wouldn't let you down.' He glanced across at his father. 'Have you tried roping in Dad for this shindig of yours? He'd make a far more impressive prize than I would.'

'Oh no, you don't!' Sir Robert dismissed the idea with raised hands. 'I give anything to do with women's clubs a very wide berth. Besides,' he added with a grin reminiscent of his son, 'I'm far too old to stand around in corners ogling young girls with the rest of the lads.'

'Robert!' His sister looked at him reproachfully and he winked at Gavin in triumph. 'Oh, there's one other thing,' Aunt Gaby remembered. 'Will you be wanting two tickets, Gavin?'

A brief, speculative glance flicked at Jane, then he smiled. 'Of course,' he told her. 'The catch of the evening can't very well come solo, can he?'

'You'll be bringing – Mrs. Dray?'

'I'll be bringing Ellen,' he agreed, and Jane's hands gripped the handle of her cup tightly.

Jane found herself facing the prospect of the Ladies'

Club dance with reluctance. She had been several times before in the old days and in Gavin's company, before he became such a celebrity as he was now. Ellen Dray, she thought wryly, would be highly delighted at being escorted by the star of the evening and no doubt that fabulous opal would come in for its share of admiration and envy.

The thought of Gavin's being engaged to Ellen only made Jane more reluctant, for it would no doubt cause quite a bout of speculation and wonder when she and Gavin each brought another partner. Gavin had so far been very discreet about his relationship with Ellen, at least in their home surroundings. They had ridden together and gone into Exeter to lunch and dinner, but most of their more intimate meetings had been in London before Ellen moved back to the farm. Very few of the people in Penford would know of their association and it would no doubt cause a good deal of gossip.

Gavin seemed to be accepting his role as top prize of the evening with his usual aplomb, but no special enthusiasm. Peter showed even less enthusiasm, but Aunt Gaby made up for them all by bustling about excitedly. She was not a woman who normally enjoyed much social activity, but she had been a member of the Ladies' Club for many years and most of the people who went to the dance she either knew personally or knew of, so that she counted it a gathering of friends.

Jane tried not to let her feelings show, for she would hate to spoil Aunt Gaby's enjoyment, but her reluctance was obvious to one person at least.

'You do want to go to this dance, I suppose?' Peter asked hopefully, a day or two before. 'If you don't, darling, for heaven's sake say so, because I don't mind in the least having a dinner for two in Exeter instead.'

For a moment Jane was tempted by the idea, then she rejected it firmly. 'Of course I want to go.' She was determined not to be talked out of it, for one thing because Aunt Gaby would be horribly disappointed and for another Ellen Dray would no doubt consider it a personal triumph if Jane stayed away. 'I like the club dance,' she told him, 'and Margaret Hannon would be awfully upset now if I didn't go after I've promised.'

Peter looked dubious. 'She's more likely to be upset if Gavin doesn't go, I should imagine,' he said, 'considering he's the big draw of the evening.' He laughed harshly and his lip curled in a way that spoke volumes. 'Good grief, how a man can allow himself to be – be publicly auctioned like that beats me. It either takes a lot of nerve or a lot of conceit, I can't decide which in this case, maybe both.'

Jane flushed, disliking not only the sneering tone he used, but the implied slight to Aunt Gaby who had arranged it. 'Public figures often have to be prepared to do a lot of things they don't enjoy,' she told him, 'and Gavin's very good at not making too much fuss about it. He's done a lot for charity since he made his name.'

She saw him frown and wondered if she had been a little too quick in her defence of Gavin, but she had spoken no more than the truth, and even the devil, she told herself, was entitled to his due.

'I suppose it's good publicity,' Peter allowed not very charitably.

'It sells a lot of tickets,' Jane agreed, deliberately misunderstanding his allusion to publicity, 'and that means more for the old folks' fund.'

'How do we dress?' he asked, with a big city's condecension for small-town activities.

'As you would for any other dance,' Jane told him, with a smile for his unconscious superiority. 'I've bought a new dress and so will everyone else. You'd be surprised,' she teased him, 'we wear dance dresses even in the wilds of Devonshire!'

He acknowledged the dig by looking slightly shame-faced, and drew her close enough to kiss her forehead. 'I'm sure you'll look like a million pounds, darling, and I'll try to live up to you. What's it like, this creation you've bought to dazzle me with?'

It was so completely unlike him to take any interest in what she wore that she smiled wryly, and it was only when she came to answer him that she realized her choice of colour had been almost instinctive and until now she had not realized its significance.

'It's very glamorous and very flattering, and it's turquoise, a lovely deep turquoise – I hope you like it.'

'I'm sure I shall if you're wearing it.' The compliment was genuine, she felt sure, but it was not accompanied, as it would have been from Gavin, by that quick gleam of triumph because she had chosen that colour. Turquoise had always been Gavin's favourite colour, especially for her, and she only now realized that she had automatically chosen it with that in mind, however unconsciously.

'You like turquoise?' She sought more definite approval and he looked a little surprised.

'Yes, yes, of course I do. It's a sort of bluey-green, isn't it? I'm not very good on colours, I'm afraid, but it sounds very nice and I'm sure it'll suit you.'

It was a small thing, she realized, but his lack of interest somehow disappointed her. A man with his mind always busy with business problems, of course, would have little time to be interested in women's clothes, even if the woman was to be his wife. It was something she would have to get used to, and quite reasonable in the circumstances. Gavin, on the other hand— She dismissed that thought firmly, almost before it entered her head.

Aunt Gaby, when she saw the dress she had bought for the occasion, smiled knowingly, much to Jane's embarrassment, for she could not fail to interpret the meaning behind the smile. 'It's lovely, darling,' Aunt Gaby told her. 'That colour always suits you so well, that's why you chose it, of course.'

To some, the remark might have sounded quite innocent, but Jane was alert for implications and she flushed, not meeting the questioning eyes that sought hers in the mirror. 'Of course, Aunt Gaby, why else?'

'No reason, dear,' Aunt Gaby replied blandly. 'It's just that I know it's Gavin's favourite colour and I always thought you chose it as much to please him as for any other reason.'

'Well, I didn't.' It was a lie and Aunt Gaby knew it, but she made no further comment, but merely smiled briefly as if in satisfaction.

'Will you wear your hair up, the way you used to?' The bright, dark gaze speculated again. 'You used to have it sort of soft and curly, much less severe than you do now.'

'I don't know.' Jane surveyed her reflection thoughtfully. She supposed her hair-style was more severe now than it used to be, but she was two years older and felt it more in keeping with her new image. 'Peter likes it this way.'

'I liked it the other way much better,' Aunt Gaby

told her persuasively. 'And with that dress, darling, I really think it would be more – more the old you, somehow.'

Jane met her gaze in the mirror. 'I'm not the old me, Aunt Gaby. I'm the new, more sophisticated, less naïve me, and I think this style will suit me as well as anything.'

'As you like, darling,' Aunt Gaby surrendered unwillingly, and Jane could not resist a smile at her expression.

When Peter eventually saw her in the dress, on the night of the dance, he was so flatteringly appreciative, more so than he had ever been before, that she could scarcely hide her surprise. She wondered, too, how much of his appreciation was prompted by Gavin's being there and by his impudent and highly provocative whistle when she walked into the room.

'You look beautiful, my darling,' Peter told her, while Gavin watched her with his deep grey eyes glowing with that expression that always made her feel as if her knees were about to give way under her.

'Thank you.' She lifted her face for Peter's kiss, trying to ignore Gavin's presence altogether, not an easy thing to do at any time and particularly when he was bent on catching her eye.

'Is that what they call turquoise?' Peter asked, unaware of the hare he was starting.

'Yes, yes, it is.' She pirouetted in front of him, the soft material of the dress swirling out round her. 'Do you like it?'

'It's very pretty,' he agreed, 'very pretty indeed.'

'You look like a sea-nymph rising out of a sea of jewels,' Gavin said softly, his deep voice quiet and undeniably seductive. 'Like Venus herself, beautiful and irresistible. That's still your colour, darling, and I'm flattered you remembered.'

There was silence for a moment and a stillness that seemed to Jane like a warning. Peter's blue gaze had a hint of that chilling iciness she hated so much and he looked from her to Gavin as if he suspected they shared some secret and were conspiring against him.

'Remembered?' he asked, an arm possessively round her shoulders, and Gavin merely smiled, leaving Jane to explain as best she could.

'It's – it's just that – well, I've worn this colour so often it's become almost a family joke,' she explained.

It was not the right answer, she realized, and Peter's frown remained. 'Then why should Gavin be flattered?' he asked bluntly, and Jane bit her lip, suddenly hating the dress and wishing she had chosen any other colour but this.

It was Gavin who supplied an answer this time and, inevitably, made things worse. 'Because it's my favourite colour,' he said softly, 'isn't it, Janty?'

For a moment Jane could find no words, but merely stood, silent and rather vulnerable, between the two of them. 'I – I'd forgotten,' she said at last. 'I just liked it, so I bought it. I – I never thought about anything else.' It was the truth, or at least she had been unconscious of any other influence, but she did not expect either of them to believe her. She raised her eyes and met Peter's, cold and doubtful, wishing with all her heart that Aunt Gaby was there to help.

It was not Aunt Gaby, however, but Uncle Robert who came in and his first words were hardly guaranteed to restore normality. 'Jane darling, you look utterly delectable in that frock. You'll be the belle of the ball – I always loved you in that colour.'

'Thank you, Uncle Robert.' Her rather subdued response brought a puzzled frown to his face and he flicked a curious glance at his son and Peter, then shrugged. 'Just off to your bunfight?' he joked.

'I'm off as soon as Aunt Gaby's ready,' Gavin told him. 'We're taking her with us.'

Aunt Gaby had decided to be driven in Gavin's car, although Jane and Peter had offered to take her with them. Gavin, who had obviously seen through her ruse and resented it not at all, had laughed and told her that she only wanted to act as chaperone to him and Ellen, a fact which Aunt Gaby had not denied and which Jane too suspected was probably the truth.

Driving along the Penford road, with the moon full and yellow in a blue-black sky Peter maintained a silence that made Jane's heart sink dismally. His jealousy of Gavin was bad enough, but she hated it when he expressed his disapproval in a heavy, reproachful silence as now.

'Peter.' She put a tentative hand on his arm and felt him stiffen under her touch. A moment later, however, he turned his head briefly and smiled at her.

'You *do* look beautiful,' he told her, 'and the moonlight suits you.'

'Thank you, kind sir.' Her smile held relief as well as pleasure. 'That's quite poetic.'

'For a business man,' he added, and managed to make it sound as if she had meant to finish the sentence that way herself.

'I didn't *say* that,' she protested, and he glanced at her again.

'But you meant it,' he insisted. 'I know I haven't Gavin's gift for words, Jane, you'll just have to get used to something a bit less flamboyant, I'm afraid, but far more sincere.'

She was unsure whether to voice the objection that came instinctively to her lips and thought it best not to, on reflection; there was no sense in encouraging that disapproving silence again, so she said nothing.

The sight and sound of the crowded hall helped to raise Jane's spirits again and she found herself looking forward to meeting old friends again, despite the possible embarrassment of being in Peter's company instead of Gavin's as before.

'It looks as if there's a good crowd,' she told Peter as they walked across the patch of rather worn grass that separated the front of the hall from the road.

'No doubt drawn by the prospect of winning Gavin as a prize,' Peter commented, and Jane would have protested but for the smile that placated her.

Margaret Hannon, an old friend of Aunt Gaby's, and this year's secretary of the host club, came across the room to meet them when she spotted Jane, her rather odd-looking face smiling anxiously. 'Jane dear! Lovely to see you again.' She looked over Jane's shoulder at the entrance hall, sparing barely a glance for Peter, who surveyed the crowded hall unenthusiastically.

'Hello, Mrs. Hannon.' She introduced Peter and saw the first spark of curiosity in the woman's eyes as she shook hands with him.

'Delighted you could come, Mr. Frith.' The fleeting gaze again sought someone following them and the smile became even more anxious. 'Jane, aren't Gaby and Gavin coming? I'm sure Gaby said that he—'

'Gavin's coming, Mrs. Hannon,' Jane assured her, 'and he's bringing Aunt Gaby. They were almost ready when we left, but they had to pick up Ellen Dray on the way here.'

'The Dunn girl?' She gave Ellen her maiden name as a lot of the local people did and the curiosity now glistened unchecked in her eyes as she looked at Jane curiously. 'I must say I was *very* surprised to hear that Gavin was bringing her. I would never have thought Gavin would settle for anyone so—' Margaret Hannon was a snob and thin hands consigned Ellen Dray to a lower social stratum. 'But still, things change, don't they?'

Jane was almost glad at that moment to see the subject of the scorn come in with Gavin and Aunt Gaby. If Ellen was less than pleased with their chaperone, she nevertheless clung with determination to Gavin's arm, her baby-blue eyes wide and glinting pleasure at being seen with him among his and his aunt's friends. It was, Jane realized, a moment of triumph for Ellen Dray.

She silently urged Peter further into the hall where they could mingle with the crowd and be less conspicuous than standing in the doorway, where Gavin's arrival was already causing heads to turn.

'Mrs. Dray looks very attractive,' Peter commented, rather tactlessly, Jane felt, but she had to allow that he was right about Ellen.

'If I were a blonde it would never have occurred to me to wear orange,' she conceded, 'but I have to admit it suits her.'

'Perhaps,' Peter suggested, soft-voiced, 'it's another of Gavin's favourite colours.'

The jibe was intentional, Jane reflected, and she flushed at it. 'It isn't, as it happens,' she retorted. 'He hates it.'

That Ellen Dray could have made such an obvious

172

mistake caused a momentary and meaningful silence, then they both laughed, though for different reasons, Jane suspected. Her own amusement, she was ready to admit, was prompted by malice when she thought of what lack of understanding there must be between Gavin and the girl who professed to know him so well.

Several times, as she danced during the evening, Jane was aware that Gavin was watching her and, finally, he managed to catch her eye, lowering one lid in a wink that expressed heaven knew what, right above Ellen Dray's confident blonde head.

Peter saw the gesture too, Jane realized a moment later, for she felt the arm about her tighten imperceptibly and saw the frown that drew his brows together. 'I could do with some air,' he told her brusequely. 'Let's go outside for a while, shall we?'

'If you'd like to.' She agreed willingly enough although she knew there was more than a sudden desire for fresh air behind the suggestion. Nevertheless it was much cooler outside and she was glad to escape herself for a few minutes.

The ground at the back of the hall was not worthy of the name garden, but there were one or two rather scrub-like trees and a patch of grass that struck pleasantly cool through her open sandals. Peter held her hand and they walked to the limit of the ground which ended at a privet hedge bordering a playing field.

'Phew! That's better.' He looked down at her. 'I couldn't stand any more of that.'

Jane half-smiled. 'The heat or the dance?'

'Both.' His answer was unexpectedly blunt and she glanced at him hastily. 'Frankly, darling, I'm not too happy at shindigs like this, and it's doubly maddening when I've to watch Gavin Blair trying to have his cake and eat it too.'

'I – I don't understand.' For some reason Jane felt taut and uneasy suddenly, as if something she had been expecting to happen was already beginning. 'I'm sorry you don't like the dance. We can go if you'd rather, although it *is* rather early and it'll look a bit odd.'

'It's up to you,' he told her. 'I admit I'd like to leave and drive somewhere quiet with just the two of us. Away from your so-called cousin's roving eye.'

'Peter!'

He set his face stubbornly, obviously not intending to retract. 'I'm sorry, my darling, but that's the way I feel. Blair's done nothing but ogle you over Ellen Dray's head all evening so far, and I'm getting sick of it.'

'I – you're wrong, Peter, you really are.' She sought to placate him, but thought she faced a losing battle when she saw the stubborn set of his jaw and the hard look in his eyes again.

'I'm not wrong,' he insisted, and turned her to face him, his fingers strong and hard on her arms. 'Listen to me, Jane. I'm going back to London the day after tomorrow and I shan't be coming back this time. I'm getting a special licence as soon as I get back and, if you *do* want to marry me, you'll be back in London on Saturday.'

'On Saturday!' She stared at him, scarcely believing she had heard aright. It was an ultimatum pure and simple and it sounded so heart-stoppingly final that she could not find words for several minutes.

Peter nodded. 'Nothing fancy or fussy, darling, just the two of us and a short, simple ceremony at the registrar's office. It's the way I want it to be, Jane, and if you love me you'll be there.'

Jane still stared, shaking her head slowly, remembering Gavin's threat that Peter would probably not give in to her so easily as he had always done. 'But – but it sounds so – so final, Peter.'

'It *is* final,' he told her, an edge of impatience on his voice. 'I love you, Jane, and I want to marry you, but on my own ground and on my terms, not here where Gavin Blair's influence can change your mind at the last minute.'

'But – but that's less than a week.' She realized ruefully that she was already seeking excuses.

'I know it is,' he said, watching her with that hard chilling look she disliked so much. He sounded so adamant that she wondered how she could ever have thought him amenable to *her* will. Then the hard eyes softened and warmed suddenly and he slid his arms round her waist, pulling her close. 'Please be there, Jane.'

He was already drawing her closer and his head was bowed over her, seeking her mouth, when Jane heard the soft swish of footsteps over the grass and hastily drew back.

Peter turned, a black frown condemning the intruder. 'I'm sorry,' Aunt Gaby ventured, as if she was loath to disturb them.

Jane gave her a smile, though a rather uncertain one. 'It's all right,' she told her. 'Is something wrong, Aunt Gaby?'

'Not wrong,' Aunt Gaby admitted, and for the first time Jane recognized a shiny gleam in her dark eyes as she looked at her. 'I just came to see if you have a yellow ticket with number twenty-five on it, darling.'

For a moment Jane stared at her, then began to riffle through the multi-coloured draw tickets that cluttered her bag. 'I'll see,' she told her, while Peter looked on impatiently.

'There's a hold-up at the moment,' Aunt Gaby explained. 'We're drawing for the various prizes and no one seems to have this yellow twenty-five, so I said I'd come and see if you had it.'

'I have.' Jane produced the required ticket and handed it over to a smiling Aunt Gaby. 'What have I won?' she asked.

It was Peter who answered before Aunt Gaby could tell her, his voice hard and bitter and the icy look in his eyes again as he looked at the old lady. 'Since Mrs. Drummond has take the trouble to come out here and find you, Jane, you have no need to ask, surely. You've won the prize of the evening – Gavin Blair.'

CHAPTER ELEVEN

IT was only to be expected that Peter would take exception to Jane's winning the one prize that could cause trouble between them. Jane had wanted to refuse, to let someone else have the privilege of Gavin's company for an evening, but Margaret Hannon, encouraged, Jane felt sure, by Aunt Gaby, had insisted that she keep it since she had won quite fairly.

She was the target of quite a few envious glances from the younger women, who had hopefully bought tickets, and Ellen Dray had glared at her so malevolently that she shivered. Between Peter and Ellen, she felt, she was being unfairly blamed for something that was not her fault and certainly not of her seeking. Gavin, inevitably, found the whole thing very amusing.

'You won't go, of course?' Peter said next morning as they walked after breakfast.

'No – no, of course I shan't.'

She must have sounded very uncertain, for he looked down at her with a frown. They were walking on the moor and the warm tranquillity of the morning was already working its magic on her, making her feel relaxed and less worried.

There was still the choice that Peter had offered her the night before and which she was still doubtful about. Saturday gave her only two days to decide whether she would follow Peter back to London and marry him in what to her seemed like indecent haste.

The limit of his patience had been reached, she

thought, and if she asked for more time or let him go back to town with only a vague request for further delay, he would never ask her again. He was not nearly as patient and amenable as he had once led her to believe, and the constant reappearance of that hard-eyed look grew more disturbing the more she saw it.

'You're very quiet.' He had one arm round her and there was only warmth and curiosity in his eyes now as he smiled down at her.

She half-smiled, curling her sandalled toes in the warm prickle of the heather. 'I have a lot to think about,' she told him.

'About us?'

She nodded, wondering if she dared suggest a further delay. 'Saturday is only two days away.'

'It's four days if you count today and Saturday,' he told her, no hint of relenting in his voice.

'It isn't very long.'

'It's long enough if you love me, Jane. I have no hesitation at all.'

'But there's Aunt Gaby. I must consider her.'

'You don't have to consider anyone but you and me,' he argued, his jaw set firm. 'We're the ones that matter, Jane, it's our lives.'

'But they're my family,' she protested, 'Uncle Robert and Aunt Gaby; it seems so – so ungrateful after all they've done for me.'

'Gavin's your family too,' Peter retorted. 'You're not suggesting we invite *him* to our wedding, are you?'

'No, of course not. Besides,' she glanced across at the silvery gleam of the tiny Medd where only a week ago Ellen Dray had so unceremoniously pushed her into the water after showing off her engagement ring,

'Gavin will have plans of his own. He won't have time to be interested in my doings.'

'Nonsense!' His vehemence startled her. 'He'll never let go while you stay on here, Jane. A complete break with all this,' he waved a derogatory hand at the surrounding moor, 'is the only way you'll ever be free of him.'

'You – you mean never come back here?'

'It's the only way, darling.'

Jane felt a chill suddenly, as if the warm golden morning had vanished and her only prospect the impersonal bustle of town. There was so much to lose if she never came back again, so many things she would miss, so much she would long for that the city could never make up for. Perhaps there *were* too many reminders of Gavin both here and at Pendart, but with him gone away again, they would recede and grow less painful, until only the soft, familiar comfort of the place remained. It was something she could not face, not a permanent severance from everything she loved.

'I – I can't, Peter!'

Her heart was in her voice and in the wide eyes that looked at him so appealingly, and he drew her close to him, his arms seeking to reassure her. 'Oh, Jane, don't look so hurt, my darling, I'll love you so much you'll forget in time, I promise you, then, when you've grown used to being away and we've made a life together, I'll bring you back here and we'll make our own memories, after the others have died.'

It sounded so simple, the way he said it, as if it could really happen. 'Please, Peter.' She raised her head from his shoulder and looked up at the same determined expression. Nothing, she told herself, had changed or ever would once Peter made up his mind to it. No matter how she pleaded he would never give in, never allow her to come here again while the memories she shared with Gavin were still rekindled each time she walked on the moor or slept in Pendart's familiar tranquillity.

'It's your choice, darling,' he told her, and Jane closed her eyes for a moment despairingly.

It was already Thursday and Jane, wide awake long before her usual time, lay watching the morning ripen, through the uncurtained windows. If only it would rain, she thought illogically, it might make her choice easier. It was impossible, while the days were so warm and wonderful, to face the prospect of never walking on her beloved moors again, but if it rained it would seem as if they wept to see her go and so made up her mind for her.

Aunt Gaby noticed her preoccupation at breakfast but, wisely, said nothing. 'You're leaving this morning, Mr. Frith,' she said to Peter. 'Shall we be seeing you again?'

Peter looked across at Jane as he answered, a look she refused to meet. 'I don't think so, Mrs. Drummond, though I'm extremely grateful to you for having me for so long.'

'As long as you've enjoyed your stay,' Aunt Gaby told him, making no comment on his finality. 'I'm sure no one can fail to enjoy the moor, it's fascinating country and very beautiful.'

Peter smiled wryly. 'It *is* lovely country, I agree, but I have to confess to being a thorough city-dweller. I miss the bustle and activity, the sense of belonging, I'm afraid.'

'Oh, but don't you ever relax?' Aunt Gaby asked, and he smiled.

'Certainly, as often as I can, but at a theatre or dinner parties, and so on, I relax, but in my own way.'

In his own way, Jane thought despairingly, but not in mine, and she almost shed the tears that prickled warningly at the back of her eyes. She stirred her coffee absently, unaware at first of Gavin watching her, then the intensity of his gaze drew her irresistibly and she looked across at him.

For a moment it seemed as if the last two years had never been, and both understanding and gentleness filled the grey eyes and comforted her, then, when she would have instinctively responded, he grinned in the old rakish way, flicking a brow upwards in query. 'Talking of theatres et cetera, *are* you coming with me on Friday night, Janty?'

She should have shaken her head and been immediate and adamant in her refusal, she knew, but instead she wavered uncertainly, biting her lower lip, leaving it to Peter to answer.

'I doubt it very much,' he told Gavin. 'I'm hoping Jane will be in London on Saturday and she'll need to start early.'

It was anticipating her decision to sound so sure of her, and Jane felt a prickle of resentment, colouring furiously under the curious gaze of three pairs of eyes. Aunt Gaby looked unbelieving and a little anxious, Uncle Robert completely puzzled, while Gavin watched her, almost daring her to answer, a dark glitter of challenge in his eyes.

'I – I may—' she began, and Aunt Gaby stretched out a reassuring hand, her bright eyes even brighter than usual with tears not too far away.

'If you are going back to London, darling, you could surely have dinner with Gavin before you go, couldn't you?' she asked.

It was almost as if she knew of Peter's ultimatum, Jane thought, almost as if she was trying, one last time, to send her back to Gavin.

'I – I could,' she agreed, and almost shouted at Peter not to frown at her so. After all, if she was never to see Gavin again or Pendart, it was surely not asking too much to let her end the association in her own way.

'You'll come?' Gavin's voice was deep and so soft, only she was meant to hear.

'Yes – I'll come.' She looked across at Peter and saw resignation as well as disapproval in his expression now.

It was some time after breakfast, just before Peter was due to leave, that Jane found him, sitting rather disconsolately on the wide gate post at the top of the garden, one foot swinging as he contemplated the wide, golden expanse of the moor. He turned his head as she approached and smiled at her, looking more like the Peter she had first known than the one she had seen of late. Something reserved and a little shy in his manner.

'I'm trying hard to absorb some of your fascination for the wide open spaces,' he told her.

'Are you succeeding?' She leaned against the gate, following his gaze to the distant hills and rivers, wondering how anyone could fail to be completely enchanted by it all.

His laugh was short and harsh and completely devoid of humour. 'I'm afraid not,' he confessed. 'I'm a town man through and through, Jane. I'll never change.'

'I – I don't know whether *I* can.' She traced a pattern on the wooden top of the gate with one finger.

'But you'll try?'

She did not answer for a moment, only stood silent and thoughtful, almost sensing the warm, tranquil moor waiting for her reply. 'I honestly would try, Peter, if I thought I could succeed, but I'm not sure I can, so perhaps it's best – best if you don't expect me on Saturday. I'd hate to – to let you down at the last minute, and I'm so afraid I may.'

To her surprise he shook his head. 'I told you once, Jane, I'd wait as long as I had to for you, and that means right up to the last minute. I shan't give up until Saturday comes. If you're not there then—' He spread his hands in a gesture of surrender and Jane felt suddenly sad and tearful again. There was something so likeable about Peter, it would be awfully hard to hurt him and she was not sure she could do it.

Dressing for her date with Gavin the following night, Jane found herself far more excited than she told herself she should be. Peter was gone and she was faced with a difficult choice, also it was not in the least like old times, for Gavin was now committed to Ellen Dray, but still she could not still the excited flutter of her pulse nor conceal the betraying glow in her eyes.

She dressed slowly and with infinite care, in a deep green dress that flattered both her golden tan and the greeny-grey of her eyes. Her hair she dressed, almost unthinkingly, in a less severe style than she had of late, so that soft tendrils of it curled and whispered against her neck and ears.

It was more like the old Jane of two years ago, she

thought wryly as she surveyed her reflection, except that there was a certain air of uneasiness behind the excitement in her eyes. She sighed deeply as she smoothed her hands over the softness of the dress before turning away. It could never be like old times again, but it would be harmless enough to pretend that it was.

Aunt Gaby nodded her satisfaction when she came downstairs and Gavin left his chair in one of the swift, smooth movements that were so typical of him, his eyes dark and appraising.

'You look lovely, darling,' Aunt Gaby told her. 'Doesn't she, Gavin?'

'Always.' The grey eyes had that look in them again that made Jane feel so weak she felt she would topple and she hastily lowered her gaze.

'Are we going alone?' she asked.

'Alone?' There was as much surprise as amusement in his look.

'I mean,' she hastened to explain, 'I – I wondered if Ellen was coming with us.'

This time he laughed, looking at her as if she had suggested something scandalous. 'Darling, what an idea! Who plays gooseberry, you or Ellen?'

Jane flushed. 'You know perfectly well what I mean, Gavin,' she said shortly, collecting her bag from a chair. 'In the circumstances your fiancée could reasonably expect to come along too.'

'Do you think so?' He shook his head, laughter not far away. 'You're a cock-eyed little devil,' he informed her. 'Come on, let's go before you drop any more clangers.'

'But—'

'Come on, Janty.' He took her arm and led her to the door, turning in the doorway to wink an eye at Aunt

184

Gaby and his father. 'Expect us when you see us,' he told them.

The moon was a little less than full tonight, but it sat, fat and yellow in a starry sky with what looked suspiciously like a smile on its face, making long, thick shadows on the road so that Gavin needed all his concentration to guide the car round the numerous curves and corners that bordered the moor on the road to Exeter.

'Isn't it a bit late to be starting out?' Jane suggested, and he shook his head, flicking her a smile that was only a flash of white in the dim interior of the car.

'No sense in starting the evening too soon,' he said. 'I like coming home in the wee sma' hours, remember?'

How could she not remember the number of times they had driven home at one and two in the morning, wide awake and deliciously alone in a quiet world. 'I remember,' she agreed.

'I thought a late supper at Sunby's,' he went on, and he must have known, she thought, what he was doing to her self-control. 'Do you remember that too?'

Sunby's was small and quiet and never seemed to close. The lighting was soft and low and guaranteed to invoke a romantic atmosphere even with the unimaginative. Jane knew it well – perhaps too well.

'No, Gavin!' She scarcely realized she had voiced the objection, but she saw his head jerk briefly in her direction and then he drew the car into the side of the road and plunged them into the softness of silence as he cut the engine.

He turned and looked at her, sitting slightly bowed in her seat, her hands clutching the little bag she held as if it could give her strength, trying to stop her hands from trembling and the tears from starting in her eyes.

'Please – take me home!' It was a cry from the heart and the first warm drop fell mournfully on to her clasped hands.

He made no answer but got out of the car and came round to open her door, his hands half lifting her from her seat, and she stood like a sleep-walker while he closed the door. Still without speaking her put an arm round her and led her to where the hedge parted and left a view of the moor that was breathtaking under the yellow moon.

He stopped and turned her face to him, keeping his hands on her arms, his eyes dark and glowing as he looked down at her. 'Now,' he said, 'we'll settle one or two things before we go any further, shall we?'

'There's nothing left to settle.' She looked and felt small and unhappy, wishing she had the strength to walk away and leave him once and for all.

He lifted her chin with one finger and she saw the flash of his smile again against his dark face. 'Like why you're supposed to be in London tomorrow?' he suggested, and she bit her lip at being reminded. 'Is it to marry him, Janty? Is that why you're supposed to be going?' Suppose, she noticed, he still would not accept that she might well go to Peter for good.

'I – I was – I mean I *am* going to—'

His laugh, soft and deep interrupted her. 'Oh *no*, my darling, you wouldn't, not while you're so uncertain.'

It was the old magic again, she thought in sudden panic, the moonlight on the moor and his deep, persuasive voice. She tried to snatch her arms away from his hold. 'Stop it, Gavin, stop it!' Her voice was scarcely audible for the choking feeling in her throat and the tears rolled unchecked down her cheeks. 'You have

no right to – to be here like this with me. You – you're
doing exactly the same to Ellen as you did to me, only I
don't find revenge very sweet. I hate it, and I hate you
for trying to – to—'

'Seduce you?' he offered, and sounded far more
calm than he had any right to be.

'You're engaged to Ellen!' She managed to steady
her voice enough to convey her scorn.

'Who told you that?'

His self-confidence made her uneasy and she stared
at him for a long moment, feeling the blood pounding
away at her temple until she could scarcely hear or see.
'She – she showed me her ring,' she explained, horribly
unsure of herself. 'An opal as big as – as a pebble.'

He smiled, shaking his head. 'Go on,' he told her,
but she hesitated, convinced now that he was only
waiting to prove her laughably wrong.

'I – I heard you,' she went on at last, remembering
that night along the Penford road when she had
hidden from them behind the hedge. 'I heard you
say—'

'I know what you heard me say,' he told her, still so
full of confidence her heart sank. 'And you thought I
was talking about something quite different. You
jumped to the wrong conclusion, as usual.'

'I—' She sought hastily for something he could not
dismiss so easily. 'That ring—' she ventured, and he
laughed softly.

'That ring,' he told her, undeterred, 'was one that
Ellen's husband left to her. I know that lately she's
taken to wearing it on – well, where it can be most
misleading, but that has nothing to do with me. As for
the conversation you eavesdropped on, your little ears
could have heard only a few sentences at most from

behind that hedge, and I wasn't talking about me and Ellen, as I suppose you thought, but about me and you.'

'Me?' She stared at him, her hands trembling so much she could do nothing about them.

'You, you cock-eyed little female.'

'But – but Ellen—' She looked at him, lips parted, eyes as big as pools and dark in the moonlight, unable to do anything about the relentless thud of her heart and the sudden exhilarating lightness in her head.

'Ellen,' he told her slowly, 'knows exactly where she stands, she always has as far as I'm concerned. She's a good friend and I know she'd like – well, we needn't go into that now. Probably she's been a bit less than tactful or charitable to you at times, but let's face it, darling, you've not exactly been friendly to her, have you?'

'I've been—' Jane began, but stopped when she met the challenge in his eyes.

'You're a stubborn, bad-tempered, spoiled little wretch,' he told her calmly, 'and I love you to distraction. I warn you I'm in no mood to be kept in suspense like poor old Peter, so I'm not *asking* you to marry me, I'm *telling* you.'

Jane was, she suddenly discovered, held breathlessly tight in his arms and there was a wonderful, comforting familiarity about the moment as he kissed her mouth, kissed her as if he would never let her breathe again.

'Gavin!'

There was just time to say his name once, before he kissed her again, and the fat yellow moon gave an endless look to the silent moor.

FREE! *Harlequin Romance Catalogue*

Here is a wonderful opportunity to read many of the Harlequin Romances you may have missed.

The HARLEQUIN ROMANCE CATALOGUE lists hundreds of titles which possibly are no longer available at your local bookseller. To receive your copy, just fill out the coupon below, mail it to us, and we'll rush your catalogue to you!

Following this page you'll find a sampling of a few of the Harlequin Romances listed in the catalogue. Should you wish to order any of these immediately, kindly check the titles desired and mail with coupon.

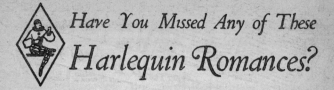

Have You Missed Any of These
Harlequin Romances?

☐ 1031 FLOWERING DESERT
     Elizabeth Hoy
☐ 1100 THE BROKEN WING
     Mary Burchell
☐ 1103 HEART OF GOLD
     Marjorie Moore
☐ 1138 LOVING IS GIVING
     Mary Burchell
☐ 1146 THE IMPERFECT SECRETARY
     Marjorie Lewty
☐ 1149 A NIGHTINGALE IN THE
     SYCAMORE   J. Beaufort
☐ 1164 MEADOWSWEET
     Margaret Malcolm
☐ 1165 WARD OF LUCIFER
     Mary Burchell
☐ 1167 DEAR BARBARIAN
     Janice Gray
☐ 1168 ROSE IN THE BUD
     Susan Barrie
☐ 1171 THE WINGS OF MEMORY
     Eleanor Farnes
☐ 1173 RED AS A ROSE
     Hilary Wilde
☐ 1181 DANGEROUS LOVE
     Jane Beaufort
☐ 1182 GOLDEN APPLE ISLAND
     Jane Arbor
☐ 1184 THE HOUSE OF OLIVER
     Jean S. Macleod
☐ 1213 THE MOONFLOWER
     Jean S. Macleod
☐ 1242 NEW DOCTOR AT NORTHMOOR
     Anne Durham
☐ 1307 A CHANCE TO WIN
     Margaret Rome
☐ 1308 A MIST IN GLEN TORRAN
     Amanda Doyle
☐ 1310 TAWNY ARE THE LEAVES
     Wynne May
☐ 1311 THE MARRIAGE WHEEL
     Susan Barrie
☐ 1312 PEPPERCORN HARVEST
     Ivy Ferrari
☐ 1314 SUMMER ISLAND
     Jean S. Macleod
☐ 1315 WHERE THE KOWHAI BLOOMS
     Mary Moore
☐ 1316 CAN THIS BE LOVE ?
     Margaret Malcolm

☐ 1317 BELOVED SPARROW
     Henrietta Reid
☐ 1318 PALACE OF THE PEACOCKS
     Violet Winspear
☐ 1319 BRITTLE BONDAGE
     Rosalind Brett
☐ 1320 SPANISH LACE
     Joyce Dingwell
☐ 1322 WIND THROUGH THE
     VINEYARDS   J. Armstrong
☐ 1324 QUEEN OF HEARTS
     Sara Seale
☐ 1325 NO SOONER LOVED
     Pauline Garner
☐ 1326 MEET ON MY GROUND
     Essie Summers
☐ 1327 MORE THAN GOLD
     Hilda Pressley
☐ 1328 A WIND SIGHING
     Catherine Airlie
☐ 1330 A HOME FOR JOY
     Mary Burchell
☐ 1331 HOTEL BELVEDERE
     Iris Danbury
☐ 1332 DON'T WALK ALONE
     Jane Donelly
☐ 1333 KEEPER OF THE HEART
     Gwen Westwood
☐ 1334 THE DAMASK ROSE
     Isobel Chace
☐ 1335 THE RED CLIFFS
     Eleanor Farnes
☐ 1336 THE CYPRESS GARDEN
     Jane Arbor
☐ 1338 SEA OF ZANJ   Roumelia Lane
☐ 1339 SLAVE OF THE WIND
     Jean S. Macleod
☐ 1341 FIRE IS FOR SHARING
     Doris E. Smith
☐ 1342 THE FEEL OF SILK
     Joyce Dingwell
☐ 1344 THE DANGEROUS DELIGHT
     Violet Winspear
☐ 1352 THE MOUNTAIN OF STARS
     Catherine Airlie
☐ 1357 RIPPLES IN THE LAKE
     Mary Coates
☐ 1393 HEALER OF HEARTS
     Katrina Britt

All books are 60c. Please use the handy order coupon.

o

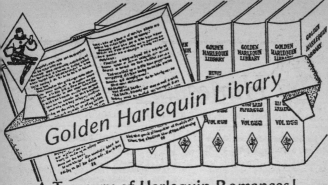

A Treasury of Harlequin Romances!

Many of the all time favorite Harlequin Romance Novels have not been available, until now, since the original printing. But on this special introductory offer, they are yours in an exquisitely bound, rich gold hardcover with royal blue imprint. Three complete unabridged novels in each volume. And the cost is so very low you'll be amazed!

Handsome, Hardcover Library Editions at Paperback Prices! ONLY $1.95 each volume.

This very special collection of classic Harlequin Romances would be a distinctive addition to your library. And imagine what a delightful gift they'd make for any Harlequin reader!

Start your collection now. See reverse of this page for **SPECIAL INTRODUCTORY OFFER!**

v